Something Old,
Something Newt

Also by Emily McVie

Newt and Improved (The Vegan Witches of Redondo Beach #2)

Everything Old Made Newt Again (The Vegan Witches of Redondo Beach #3)

Newt so Fast (The Vegan Witches of Redondo Beach #4)

Newt Kid in Town (The Vegan Witches of Redondo Beach #5)

Get this free short story when you sign up for the latest newts!

Join the vegan witch email list at **bit.ly/veganwitch**

Everything is going great for the vegan witches until their happy magical lives are thrown sideways by a hex, a barking dog, and a bad haircut.

How can they stop the hex?

Will that dog ever shut up?

Most importantly, where do they find a magic spell powerful enough to undo a bad haircut?

Something Old, Something Newt

A novel of mystery and magic

Emily McVie

The Vegan Witches of Redondo Beach

Book 1

A Wordpl**o**y Book

Acknowledgments — Thanks to Pam Eaken, David Castle, and Ed Teja for your magical help in creating this book.

Cover by Elizabeth Mackey
www.elizabethmackeygraphics.com

ISBN: 978-1-7360668-0-5

Dedicated to Mom

Chapter 1

Just as I'm beginning to think being a witch might be fun, I find a dead guy in my herb garden. The herbs are way in the back of my plant nursery — five acres of plants with a café nestled in a grove of trees at the front. Most people come for a bite at the café and shop for whatever plants are flowering. Few shoppers come all the way back to the herb garden, so I suppose it's a good place to kill a person.

How anybody can scream when they discover a corpse is beyond me. It was all I could do to hang on to my breakfast, especially after I noticed I was standing too close. One of my Converse sneakers was in the man's blood.

Blood, yes. This man did not keel over from a heart attack. He did not die a natural death. I'm new at being a witch, so I'm no expert on magic. I'm for sure no expert on murder. But standing there in my herb garden, looking down at the dead man, it was easy to see he died a very unnatural death.

I managed to keep from gagging and ran for the nursery's front desk. Sprinting by the rows of plants, I shot glances back and forth through the green leaves and colorful blooms. Was that a face on the other side of the oleander? Were eyes peering back at me?

Looking across tables of potted annuals, I strained to see if the murderer was still around. Anyone could be hiding in the ceanothus bushes, behind the lemon trees. What if he was watching me? Or she? What if several people were plotting here, for goodness sake? What if they tried to ambush me? Kill me?

I ran faster. My sneakers skidded on loose gravel as I came around the potted palms.

Panting by the time I reached the front desk, I yanked my phone off the charger, and dialed 911 while running toward the café. My friend and fellow witch Skylar runs the café. She was setting up for lunch. A woman was sitting at a table by the front window. Nobody else was there at 9:30 on a Tuesday morning. Waving frantically at Skylar, I told the 911 dispatcher I'd found a dead man in my herbs.

Skylar's eyes went wide when I pointed at the phone and mouthed "911." I tugged her with me toward the back of the nursery. She knew more about magic than I did, and I wanted her to see the dead man before the police arrived. She wasn't going to like it. She's even more squeamish about icky things than I am.

When we reached the far end of the nursery, I pointed to the body sprawled halfway into the herbs.

"Aw, God," she said, and turned away. She looked at me, her face a little green. "That's disgusting. Why'd you make me look at that?"

"You have to look at his head. You have to."

"Why? I don't want to."

"I think he was killed with magic. The police won't know what to make of it."

"He was obviously killed with that big wooden stake through his heart! I think the police will understand that really well. Way better than me."

"Skylar, the top of his head is twisted like one of those fancy light bulbs they put in chandeliers."

Skylar shook her head like she was no-way-ever going to look. Then, she shot a peeved look at me before spinning on her heels and ducking her head to look straight at the dead man's head for one second.

Facing me again, she said, "You're right. His head is messed up. Is the hair singed off one side? And what's that pool of black stuff that seems hot?"

"Hadn't noticed the black stuff. But what about the shape of his head?"

We both spun quickly to take another squinty look. When we turned back away from the body, we found two Redondo Beach police officers staring at us. That was bad enough, but their pistols were also staring at us. Skylar and I held our hands out from our sides to show that our hands weren't up to anything.

One of the officers motioned us aside. She stepped past us toward the body. The other officer watched us and spoke into a microphone on his lapel. The officer behind us said something into her radio I couldn't understand, some kind of cop code, and after a pause said, "This man is extremely dead."

The officer standing in front of us seemed to get some kind of signal from the officer behind us, because he slid his weapon into its holster. I started breathing again and let my arms relax. The man pulled a tablet computer out of a case strapped to his thigh. He touched the screen several times, studied it, and asked, "Is one of you Hayley West?"

I swallowed and raised my hand.

He looked at Skylar and asked, "And you are?"

"Skylar Bemis."

The officer touched the screen a few more times. As he messed with the tablet, figures in dark clothes moved around the nursery, lots of them, lots of cops. They were everywhere. They had to act like the killer was hiding somewhere. That didn't mean the killer was hiding somewhere. No, it didn't. Surely the killer was gone?

"Ms. West, you discovered the body?"

"I — I did," I said, startled back to reality.

"Did either of you disturb it in any way?"

We both shook our heads. "We hardly wanted to even look at it," Skylar told him.

"Yes, noticed that."

"Actually," I said, "I accidentally stepped in the man's blood when I first saw the body. If that counts as disturbing anything."

The officer didn't look up from his tablet. "Noticed the blood on your shoe," he said.

Was there anything this guy didn't notice? Could he tell we were witches?

Behind us, the officer who was examining the body said, "Hernandez, take a look."

"Pardon me ladies," he said, walking around us toward the body. "Stay exactly where you are."

He conferred with the other officer. I heard "I wonder what the pathologist will make of this." The male officer, Hernandez, said something about "Cucinelli sport coat...Neiman Marcus. That's worth about three thousand right there — or was before that stake went through it."

"You shop at Neiman's nowadays?" the female officer asked.

Hernandez said, "That guy in vice, Hammersmith, had a Cucinelli right before they busted him for the dope thing. He actually bragged to the rest of us about having a sport coat he couldn't possibly afford on a cop's salary."

The female officer said, "So how about this dead guy? Did he brag to the wrong people about having this swell jacket?"

"Or maybe that little blue Maserati in the parking lot," Hernandez added.

"No ID that's easy to get to. Don't want to mess with him too much before Nakamura gets here. When will he show up?"

"He's a last-responder."

The female officer spoke to someone on the radio about Detective Nakamura.

Officer Hernandez came back around in front of us. "Did you know this man?"

We both shook our heads that we didn't know him and both started saying that we did kind of know him.

"He ate in the café from time to time," Skylar said. "He came in with that actress, Melanie Gosford. I think he might have originally met her in the café."

"Melanie Gosford? Should I know her?"

"You would if you watched *The Young and the Restless* every day."

"Oh, a soap," officer Hernandez said dismissively.

"Daytime drama," Skylar insisted. She's a little defensive about her *Young and Restless* addiction.

"I saw him earlier this morning," I said. "Saw him yelling at someone, actually. Johnny, the guy who delivers for T-Y." Skylar and I exchanged a look. Nothing magic about Johnny. He was just a common everyday jerk.

"T-Y? The plant company?" Hernandez asked.

"Plant wholesaler, right."

He tapped the screen of his tablet and peered at it. "So this nursery is called Origins. 'Café, plants, illuminations.'" He looked at me. "You own this nursery?"

I nodded. "I run the nursery, and Skylar runs the café. Officer Hernandez, could I ask if you've ever seen a man's head look like that?" I inclined my head toward the dead guy without looking at the dead guy.

At that moment, two people wearing white hazmat suits and purple gloves went past us toward the body. Hernandez watched them. After a minute, one of the hazmat guys must have given him a look. He frowned in their direction and shrugged. Looking back at me, he said, "Have not seen anything like that. None of us. I assume his head wasn't shaped funny from the get-go?"

Before Skylar and I could tell him that the man had been thoroughly good-looking when he was alive, a man in a gray suit appeared and waved an ID in the air. "Detective Nakamura," he said. He asked Hernandez to take Skylar and me to the café and wait for him while he talked to the pathologist. "And I wonder if this café has coffee?"

"Decaf or regular?" Skylar asked automatically.

But Detective Nakamura was already talking with one of the people in the hazmat suits.

In the café, Johnny, the plant delivery guy, was sitting at a table. The woman who'd been sitting at the window earlier was still there. An older couple I didn't recognize was at another table. These must be the only people the police had rounded up from the nursery. An officer was watching over them. Hernandez explained to him that we were to wait for Nakamura and make coffee. "Regular," he told Skylar.

We went into the kitchen and whispered while we filled two big urns with water.

"So you got a good look at his head?" I asked Skylar.

She puffed out her lips. "I hate to think of that while I'm dealing with food."

"Coffee isn't food. Deal with it."

"Okay, okay. Yes, it looked like he was attacked with some bad magic. Did you get a look at that pool of black stuff?"

"I could feel the heat from it on my face. What is that stuff?"

"Pool of hot black stuff, I'd say."

I tapped my fingernail on my urn 10 times, counting. Her mother was a witch, so Skylar knew a lot about magic. I hadn't grown up with magic and didn't know much. I knew even less about my mother. Most of what I'd learned about being a witch I'd learned from Skylar in the past couple of years, but sometimes I needed to be patient. "So we have a pool of hot black stuff in our little establishment, which means the La Brea Tar Pits are coming up in Redondo Beach?"

"Different kind of black, wasn't it? And hotter."

"Magic?"

"Your guess is as good as mine." She looked at me and arched one eyebrow.

"What do we do now?" I was hoping she knew some magic way to fix everything. Her answer was the opposite of that.

"We have a chat with Detective Nakamura," she said. I looked in the direction she was looking and saw the detective standing in the doorway, tapping his pursed lips, looking at us.

"Detective!" I said by way of greeting. "The coffee will be a few minutes."

"Do you have an office?" he asked. "Someplace private where we can talk." With his dark eyes and black mustache, he seemed to be painted in ink. His close-cropped hair was a little gray at the temples.

As I passed him at the doorway he inclined his head slightly, as though he were bowing. I led the way to my little office behind the nursery's front desk. He motioned me in ahead of him and closed the door as I sat down behind my desk.

I'm not a desk person, but I always feel like I'm in charge when I'm sitting behind my desk. I looked over my laptop computer at Detective Nakamura. I'm 5'5", tall enough to see most of his face over the laptop. That seemed good enough to me.

He put a small notebook on his side of the desk and looked at me. Then, he stood up and with no change of expression slid the laptop to one side of the desk. He studied me as he took a yellow pencil out of his jacket pocket.

Picking up the palm-sized river stone on my desk, I cradled it in my hand. It always calmed me. Usually it did. I laid it back on my desk with a thunk.

Detective Nakamura said, "Let's go back to earlier this morning, when you came to work. What time was that?"

I told him, and he asked about every tiny detail of my morning after that. If I had burped, he wanted to know about it. Eventually, I told him about Johnny delivering plants. "That was the only unusual event. We got a big shipment of plants, and it's a Tuesday. Usually we get shipments on Thursdays."

"Why the change?"

"No idea, really. The girl from T-Y called yesterday and asked if they could deliver today instead."

He wrote in his notebook with the yellow pencil.

"One other fact you should know was that I saw the dead guy — who wasn't dead yet, of course — ripping a new one for Johnny. Which is not hugely unusual, because Johnny has a talent for annoyance. So Johnny probably wanted to roll his dolly where the dead guy was standing or something. And the dead guy took exception. And that's all…" I stopped. I saw that Detective Nakamura was writing with one hand and holding his other hand in the air.

When he finished writing, he looked up and said, "Let's go back to ripping a new one. What was Johnny doing just before that?"

"He was rolling in pallets of plants on a dolly, a pallet truck, taking them to the holding area at the back of the nursery."

"And what exactly was Johnny doing 10 seconds before his interaction with the victim?"

"Did not see that. When I came to the front desk, they were already talking. Well, 'the victim' was doing all the talking."

Detective Nakamura heard me putting quotes on "the victim," and said, "The victim's name is Lucan Gunter. Did you see what he was doing just before interacting with Johnny?"

"The first I saw of him this morning was when he was in Johnny's face."

"You'd seen him before today?"

"He had come in a few times. I think he met his girlfriend in the café. Met her for the first time, I mean."

"You know his girlfriend?"

"It's more like we know *of* her. Melanie Gosford. She comes into the café from time to time. Sometimes buys plants. She lives in Redondo Beach." I was pretty sure Detective Nakamura wasn't a *Young and Restless* fan, so I added, "She's on a soap. An irregular character."

"Did you see her here this morning?"

"Nope. Just him."

We heard a knock on the door, and Detective Nakamura said "Come in," before I could. I shrugged to myself. *Mi casa, su casa.*

Skylar came in with two coffee mugs. She put one down for the detective. He said, "Ah. Thank you, Ms?"

"Bemis. Skylar Bemis."

"Skylar runs the café," I told him.

He made a note and waited for Skylar to leave before asking me, "Did you hear what Lucan was saying to Johnny?"

"No. The dead guy — Lucan, I mean — was right in Johnny's face and talking under his breath. But forcefully. He was a little red in the face."

"How did Johnny react to this?"

"He was *very* red in the face. He looked like he was barely restraining himself. Lucan was several inches taller than Johnny, so Johnny was outmatched, really. And Johnny has had run-ins with other people in the past. If it happens again, he'll lose his job. So he knows he has to behave. I mean, he behaves like a jerk. But he doesn't confront people the way he used to, not for a long time now."

"Any idea why Lucan might confront him?"

"None whatsoever. It was probably nothing."

"You have some reason to protect Johnny Walen?"

"You going to 'bad cop' me now, Detective Nakamura?"

He was looking at me with the same expression he'd worn since I first saw him. Then, for a moment, I thought he was going to smile. That moment passed. He took a sip of coffee and put the mug down. "What's your relationship to Johnny Walen?"

Shrugging, I said, "He's a guy who delivers plants to me. And I don't believe he could kill somebody. Just a feeling I have."

"Just a feeling."

That was lame, but I couldn't very well tell him that Lucan had been killed with magic, and there was nothing magic about Johnny. A killer who did have magic might be lurking around the nursery, and I wanted the police to catch that person. Otherwise, I'd have to do it myself.

"Look, Detective Nakamura…"

"Ken."

"What?"

"Kennedy Nakamura. It's my name."

Bad cop, now good cop?

"Okay, Ken, look." I stopped. Was I going to say this dead guy Lucan was made dead by magic, not jerkiness? Instead, I said, "You're the professional here. I only want to point out that a killer is lurking around my nursery, and I'm sure it's not Johnny. So if your main suspect is Johnny, that leaves me with a killer lurking around my nursery."

"We will find this killer, Ms. West. We understand more than you think."

Okay, that didn't make me feel better. Really, as a witch, I'd prefer that he misunderstood me to a certain extent.

He was looking at me as if I were clear as glass, with the same expression he'd worn since I first saw him. I was getting a little tired of that expression. Why couldn't he at least frown from time to time? I mean, literally frown. I *felt* as though he was frowning all the time. Maybe it was the little downturned mustache. Maybe it was the unblinking eyes that seemed to doubt everything I said.

"What I need from you," he said, "is a clear report of what you saw and heard this morning."

He walked me through finding the body, calling 911, and dragging Skylar back to the herb garden. I couldn't very well tell him I wanted her to see the body so she could figure out what kind of magic was involved. I told him I got over-excited when I saw the body and called her to see.

"Morbidly fascinating, isn't it?"

My mouth fell open a little at that one. "Ick," I said.

"Any idea why someone might drive a stake through his heart? Like he's a vampire?"

"You think he's a vampire?" I blurted out.

Detective Nakamura and I stared at each other. And then his eyes crinkled up. His lips pressed together. He was trying not to smile. I had wanted to see his expression change, and I got it. All I had to do was make a complete fool of myself by acting like the dead guy could actually be a vampire.

Skylar hadn't told me anything about vampires. Do vampires really exist? The barely suppressed smile on Detective Kennedy Nakamura's face told me he thought not.

I found out a few years ago that I was a witch, so why not vampires? Anything was possible, including the fact that Detective Nakamura would never, ever, take me seriously again.

He stood up and slipped his yellow pencil into his jacket pocket. "Thank you, Ms. West. The nursery is now a crime scene, so it will have to remain closed until we can thoroughly check the area. You and your employees must stay out. I'll have officers keep watch on the place."

"The new plants that came this morning need watering right away. Is it okay if I do that before closing up?"

"I'm afraid not. Mustn't touch anything. Evidence could be anywhere."

He left my office and headed back to the café, probably to interview Skylar and Johnny. I knew that he wasn't going to find the evidence of magic that could solve this case. Could Skylar and I find it? We had to try. I had a back door into the nursery, and I fully intended to use it.

Chapter 2

It's a little known fact that one of the Salem witches was an actual witch. Most of the women accused of being witches were average housewives. They didn't know a magic bean from a cow, according to Skylar's mother. But in the rollicking hysteria of an otherwise dull July, 1692, the Salem judges accidentally laid their hands on a genuine witch named Sarah Good, who was accused of hexing her neighbor's husband to fall in love with her (possibly true, according to Skylar's mother). Before she was hanged, this witch cursed author Nathanial Hawthorne's great-great-grandfather, who was one of the judges at the witch trials.

Skylar's mother offered two takeaways from these events: First, witches need to keep their heads down and not attract attention. Second, human beings sometimes go haywire and hurt other human beings, and there was only so much you could do about it. This was the basic rule of thumb: Keep your head down and don't attract attention.

That approach wasn't working for Skylar and me. The bizarre murder attracted lots of attention. We were happy enough to close the café and nursery for a while, and hope the interest would fade after a few days.

This was like being a kid and hoping your mother would get over the electrifying new haircut you gave the family dog. The public's interest in a murder victim who had a stake driven through his heart had no limits. It didn't help that the *L.A. Times* referred to the case as "the so-called vampire murder." Yeah, *L.A. Times*, "so-called" by you, you bunch of annoying dimwits. Don't you know there's no such thing as vampires?

I felt like an idiot every time I thought of my conversation with Detective Nakamura. I could picture him laughing with his buddies at the police station over the vampire thing. I could hear him thinking I was the biggest dimwit in town.

And no, I can't read people's minds. However, I can talk to rocks.

"Talking to rocks" is not entirely accurate. It's more like I feel sensations that surge and ripple through stone. When I was a little girl, I could put my hands on a stone and release a question into it like dropping a pebble into a pool of water. Then, I "heard" the reverberations in the stone, flutters or shudders coursing in reply.

It's simpler to think of it the way Skylar does: Vulcan mind meld with rocks.

Skylar decided I was a witch when she saw me meld with rocks. It happened while we were in college at Fresno State. We were on an outing with other students in the nearby Sierra Nevada mountains, where thunderstorms left us stuck indoors. Beer-assisted arguments flared among a few students, and one of the guys, Gregor, stalked off all angry and sulky. As dusk approached, he still hadn't come back. We looked for him and gave up as it got dark. We called the police. They told us they'd get a search underway in the morning; nothing anybody could do in the dark.

We worried about Gregor all night, especially when more thunderstorms boomed around us. At first light, mountain rescue teams arrived and fanned out across the area. The overnight rain had obliterated Gregor's tracks. We students sat indoors and left the search to the experts. We fretted. We argued about the argument that had sent Gregor on his sulky walk.

Noon approached with no sign of Gregor, while more thunderstorms built across the sky from the west. That's when I snuck off to find a place where I could talk to the rocks. People swarmed all over the place, and aircraft crisscrossed overhead. It took me half an hour to find a place away from the search parties.

I had to find a secluded place. To meld with small rocks, I could put my hands on them and feel the waves. For a mountain of stone, I had to use more than my hands. I found a flat area of rock surrounded by pines, where I stripped off my clothes so I could lay my entire body against the bare rock.

Now, it takes a lot of patience to talk to rocks. My Uncle Ernie used to be a slow talker, but that's nothing compared to a big rock. I lay face down on that cold, wet slab of rock for what seemed like forever, nudging out ripples of question, listening for "news" of Gregor's anger. Fortunately, rocks are good at feeling anger and fear.

Unfortunately, rocks go into a tizzy of ecstatic giggling when struck by lightning. If you think that getting lit up by a quarter of a million volts doesn't sound like fun, you are not a rock. The mountains tittered and barked with hilarity as lightning flashed and thunder boomed. Was I about to be fried while the granite laughed? Wind flailed at the pine trees around my little clearing. Rain pounded down on me. The rain turned to hail.

All in all, it was not a nice day for lying bare-assed on a rock.

After an hour and a half of punishment on that cold, wet slab of rock, I tried to get up. I was chilled to the bone, shaking and turning blue. How could Gregor have made it through the night?

I got to my knees. The rain and hail had stopped, but the little pile of clothes beside me were soaked. I struggled to get to my feet and fell back to one knee, shivering. What could I do now with what I knew? How far could I walk? Could I even stand? I'd never get far enough.

Then Skylar came striding out of the trees toward me. She carried a huge plastic garbage bag. When she got to me, she pulled out a blanket and put it around me. She lifted me to my feet and wrapped her arms around me. I leaned against her, shaking.

"You know where Gregor is," she whispered in my ear. It was a statement, not a question. How could she possibly understand? I nodded twice. I wasn't sure he was still alive. If he was still breathing, it was too faint for me to get a clear answer from the rocks. But I had an impression of the way he'd walked. My teeth were chattering. Even if I could describe the way, I couldn't speak. I had to walk it.

Skylar held me up. We staggered out of the little clearing and squeezed through a cleft between house-sized boulders. A little farther on, we reached a ledge where Gregor had slipped down a slope of loose gravel. We could see him 30 yards down the slope. He was wedged between two rocks. I was barely able to move, and Skylar didn't dare try going down the loose gravel. We would have to go back for help and hope Gregor was still breathing when help arrived.

Without a word, Skylar leaned me against the rock face. She knelt on the ledge and put her palms on the loose scree. After a minute, green tendrils sprouted up through the rocks. Vines curled across the slope, this way and that, weaving a green mat downslope from where she knelt. It was a living path to Gregor. It was the most astonishing thing I had ever seen.

Skylar tested the slope and found it solid enough. She clambered down the mat of vines. When she reached Gregor, she pulled him out from between the rocks and put her arms around him the way she had me a few minutes earlier. She turned around and pulled him up the slope backwards, his heels dragging in the vines.

When she got to the top, she sat Gregor down and stayed bent over with her hands on her knees, taking deep breaths. She looked at me. "He's alive," she gasped. "I'll be back." She put her arms under his and dragged him along the ledge and out of sight.

Later, we heard he was in bad shape, nearly dead from hypothermia. But we got him out in time to save his life.

Over the next week at school, Skylar and I barely spoke. I avoided her. Something weird had happened. It scared me. Talking to rocks had seemed natural, normal. I'd always done it, though I knew other people would think it odd, and honestly, I'd often thought I might be imagining both halves of the stony conversation. Finding Gregor changed all that. The rocks really did speak to me. I really did hear what they said. Even stranger, Skylar had commanded plants to grow where she wanted them.

After a week of avoiding her, Skylar chased me down and invited me to spend the weekend with her family in Angels Camp, a town about 150 miles from Fresno. I knew she was gay. Was she making a play for me? How weird could this get? She smiled and said, "Come on. I want you to meet my mother."

That weekend, Skylar's mother took me for a walk, asked me to talk to the rocks behind their house, and told me I was a witch.

I could have thought, finally, here's someone who understands me. That wasn't my first thought. Standing there at the edge of the forest, my hand on a boulder, I didn't feel like I'd come to a place of relief or understanding. I felt like she had just told me my whole life would be weird. I didn't want to be weird.

I couldn't even be a normal witch. Skylar and I were vegan. We said no to the eye of newt and toe of frog that most spells called for. Why couldn't we at least be weird in a normal way?

My life up till then had been abnormal enough. Separated from my mother, raised by nannies in my father's big house in Connecticut, I wanted a normal life with two or three perfect children and a husband who came home every evening and told me he loved me. Who was going to love a witch?

Two years later, I'm still adjusting to "being witchy," I don't have a husband, and there's a dead guy in my herbs.

Chapter 3

Skylar and I holed up at home the day of the murder, ignoring the news reporters who came to our door. The two of us shared a small house that came with the nursery. We sat indoors, watching the news, working on a spell that might protect us from evil magic by turning the attacker's magic against them. We hoped it would be like Judo or Kung Fu — Magic Fu. Without someone to try it on, we had no idea if the spell would work.

We needed an evil witch or sorcerer to experiment on, and that's exactly what we were afraid we'd get at any moment. What kind of magic person were we up against? What kind of magic killed Lucan Gunter in the herb garden?

When it got dark, Skylar fetched a pair of pliers and we went out to the backyard. We stood by the back fence for a while, letting our eyes adjust, listening to the crickets. We couldn't hear a sound from the nursery on the other side of the fence.

After a few minutes Skylar walked backward into the shed in a corner of the yard and smashed out one of its windows with the pliers. The shattered glass fell on the grass. I could see the faint light from the sky reflected in the jagged pieces.

"I think this is the biggest piece," I said, picking up a big shard and dropping it back on the grass. "Ow, crap. Cut myself."

Skylar picked up the shard with the pliers. "Smear some of your blood on the glass."

"What?"

"The spell requires human blood."

"You didn't tell me that."

"I figured one of us would cut ourselves on the glass, so it would take care of itself."

I smeared my blood on the glass. "What happened to the idea of using vegan ingredients?"

"You're vegan."

Something about that didn't seem right. "Anyway, why do we have to use a freshly broken piece of glass?"

"If you ask *Why* questions about spells, we'll be here all night. I'll tell the story that powers the spell."

> Once upon a time, a blacksmith was making nails. He planned to use these nails to build a house for his new wife, for he was about to be married.
>
> The smith was a jealous man. He had made a deal with a shape-shifting imp to put magic in each nail. The magic would infuse the iron when the smith quenched each red-hot nail in a bucket of water taken from a nearby pool. This magic would keep his wife secure in the house and prevent other men from entering.
>
> When he had quenched the last nail, the smith walked backward into his old house and knocked out the house's only glass window with his forge pliers. He picked up the biggest piece of glass with his pliers, cut his finger on it, and smeared the blood across the glass. He carried the shard to the pool from which the imp had drawn the water for quenching the nails. Bladderwort grew in this pool. Plucking up one of the tiny sacs in which the plant

captured insects, he smeared the contents across
the glass.

Peering through the shard of glass, he saw that
the imp had fulfilled his part of the deal. The nails
glowed with magic.

"That makes no sense," I said.

Skylar shrugged. "If it made sense, it wouldn't be magic."

We walked to the tall cedar fence at the back of the yard. I
unlocked the wooden gate that opened directly into the nursery's
herb garden. The murder had happened in the place where we
worked and practically in our backyard.

We stepped through the opening and listened. The police were
supposed to be guarding the place. Were they inside the nursery or
only out front? We didn't hear anything.

Skylar carried the glass shard to a series of big plastic tubs where
I had bladderwort growing. I plucked a bladder off one and
smeared its contents across the glass.

"This is half-digested insect goo," I said. "Nothing about this
spell is vegan."

"The only other spell Mother could suggest calls for snakes and
baby birds."

"Why does magic have to be so icky?"

"Maybe it doesn't — if we can figure out vegan stuff that
works."

"If we weren't busy finding a murderer."

Skylar held up the shard of glass. We peered through it at the
herb garden. Near the spot where Lucan Gunter had died,
something was glowing bright orange. We edged closer. A faint
blue glow glimmered in the herbs and on the concrete walkway
next to the plants.

"That blue stuff is the blood," Skylar whispered. "Mother said
human blood always glows blue."

"What about that pool of orange? I'm guessing that's the hot
black stuff we saw just after the guy was killed."

"Why didn't the police take that as evidence?"

"Wouldn't fit in an evidence bag? Or they didn't realize it was evidence."

"Definitely evidence of magic," Skylar said. She squatted down and looked at it up close through the shard of glass. "This really doesn't tell us much more than that. It's magic. But what is it?"

I knelt next to her and put my hand on it. "Aehhh!" I yelled. I jerked back my hand.

"Shhh. What's wrong?"

"It's stone." I stood up and backed away a step. "It's shrieking. Like it's being tortured."

Skylar touched the stone gingerly. "I don't feel anything; just smooth, hard something or other."

She wasn't able to talk to stone, but plants she could do. She put her hands on a couple of the herbs closest to the stone. "The plants over here got very hot. They were almost scorched. I think this stone was molten at some point. Either it melted here or was molten when it fell here. But I don't think it melted before it fell, because it's all in one neat round lump."

She straightened up and we stood there in the dark trying to think of some reason why a rock would appear in our herb garden and melt on the spot.

While we were lost in thought, something touched my bare leg. I jumped and yelped.

"Shhh! What now?"

"Cat," I said, realizing the touch had been furry. I could see the orange shape now over by a planter. This cat had adopted us a few months before. We'd named her Saffron. She was friendly, customers liked her, and she kept other neighborhood cats out of the nursery. Sometimes, other cats attacked the plants for no reason I could figure out.

"Let's get out of here before the cops hear you yowling," Skylar said. "I can't think of anything else to do here. That pool of stone is baffling."

"Makes no sense," I agreed.

"Well, it is magic."

"The side of the dead guy's head was scorched."

"So a chunk of rock fell from the sky and hit him in the head? A meteor?"

"Followed by a wooden stake that went through his heart?"

"Seems far-fetched even for magic," Skylar said. "Do you think you could get anything else out of that stone?"

"I'm not putting my hands on that thing again. We have to do something for it."

"Do something for it?"

"Soothe it somehow. It's in so much pain."

"I can ask Mother if she has a painkiller for rocks. I'm sure she'll come up with half a dozen."

"Not. So we'll have to invent something."

"Good, another item on our list of vegan spells to invent."

# # #

Why didn't Hogwarts have evening classes for adults? That was the first question I asked Skylar after her mother told me I was a witch.

"Wish I'd had a school like that when I was a kid," she said. "But it could never exist in the real world. Witches and sorcerers are more disorganized than everybody else and generally distrust one another. A lot of them use magic to take advantage of other people, especially the sorcerers."

"Should I be worried about your father?" I asked.

"Only when he goes into the kitchen to make supper."

"So not all sorcerers are evil," I pointed out.

"Some are just bad cooks," she admitted. "But you know how men are. Then add magic on top of that? Not a good mix."

Yeah, Skylar wasn't fond of men. My current boyfriend wasn't magic. By that I mean he wasn't a sorcerer, and he also wasn't, you know, *magic*.

Could I do better? I hardly had time to think about it, what with running the nursery and learning about magic.

At this point I knew that witches usually have one "power" that comes naturally. In my case, it was talking to rocks. Skylar could talk to plants and had learned to control them, though it took a lot out of her.

Other powers required stories and potions, and almost all of the potions called for eye of newt, toe of frog, fang of viper, or some other icky ingredient I didn't want to deal with.

Skylar and her mother were unwilling as well, but they felt like they should teach me how it worked. Let me just say this once to be clear about the eye of newt thing: squishy, gooshy eye business. Icky ick uck yuck. That's just the beginning, because a reasonable potion needs several slimy ingredients. Lots of uck dealing with that.

Not me. I'm a vegan witch.

Chapter 4

The morning after the murder, our doorbell rang a little before 7:00. I went to look through the peephole in the front door, cursing the reporters for starting early (cursing in a sweary way, not a witchy way). It turned out to be Detective Nakamura.

I opened the door a foot and looked around it. "Detective," I said, "you're starting early."

"With apologies. I was at the nursery looking for something and wanted to ask you about a couple of items. If I may."

Reluctantly, I opened the door a little further. As he came in, he eyed my *Finding Nemo* bathrobe up and down. I think he actually blushed. Skylar gave me this robe. It was made for a child. I'm not very big, but the robe was short and tight on me. Skylar said it looked good on my tight little buns. I would have thrown it in the back of the closet, but my boyfriend loved it.

I called out to Skylar that Detective Nakamura was here.

"Ask him if he wants a scone," she shouted from the kitchen.

"He does," the detective shouted back.

After showing him into the kitchen, I went to put on some clothes. When I came back, they were sitting at the table with crumbs on their chins.

"I never imagined a vegan scone could be so good," he said.

"Skylar is a wiz at food," I told him, without mentioning that her ability to talk to plants carried over into magically good vegan cooking.

The detective finished the last bite of scone, and I took his plate to the sink. He pushed his chair back from the table a couple of inches.

"We've had several officers combing the nursery for Lucan Gunter's car keys," he said. "Did either of you happen to see them on the scene?"

We shook our heads no.

"The perp apparently emptied Gunter's pockets, including his wallet. Except this was in his jacket pocket." The detective took a plastic bag out of his own jacket pocket and handed it to me. "I'm wondering if you can tell me what it is."

The evidence bag had another plastic bag inside it. Inside that inner bag was a green plant, complete with roots and dirt. I held it closer to the light. "It's an herb in the tannis family. I'll need to take it out of these bags to be more specific."

Detective Nakamura nodded.

When I took out the inner bag and opened it, a distinctive smell wafted to my nose. It was a little like cloves. I plucked off a leaf and put it in my mouth.

"You're eating evidence," he said.

"Sorry, I just need to confirm what it is." But I already knew from the smell. "Tannis Beltane. It's an herb from the islands of Orkney that blooms on May 1st."

"Your herb garden has a hole in it where that plant used to be. How is it none of your herbs are labeled?"

"The garden is open to the public. The previous owner had trouble with people wandering through, plucking leaves for some herbal remedy they'd read about. People are less willing to take a chance on a plant that's not labeled."

"The botanists I consulted were quite impressed with your collection. That specimen you're holding baffled them."

"It's rare."

"Dangerous?"

"Ah, no. Not poisonous, if that's what you mean." I wasn't about to tell him that Tannis Beltane was the most powerful magic herb I'd found. It could only be kept alive off the Orkney Islands by magic — in this case, Skylar's plant magic. I was careful to avoid looking at her.

"Any idea why Lucan Gunter would put that in his pocket?"

I shrugged. "If he knew what it was, he could have been stealing it. That plant is worth several hundred dollars."

"To whom?"

"Oh, someone who wanted to concoct an herbal remedy with it."

"What's it good for?"

"Some people say it cures the common cold," I lied.

"Have you tried it?"

"For a cold? No, I have other herbs that don't cost so much. I can't afford much of this plant, and I wonder if I can get this one back before it dies?"

"Apologies. Evidence." He gathered the plastic bags.

Before he could put them in his pocket, Skylar asked, "Can I smell that?"

He hesitated.

"Is that the one that smells like cloves?" she asked.

He opened the inner bag and took a sniff. He handed her the bag. She held it to her nose and made a big show of smelling it. "That's the one." She handed back the bag.

Detective Nakamura tucked the bag into his jacket pocket and took out his phone. He looked at me. "I'm curious about your 911 call. The transcript includes some comments that I don't understand." He read from his phone, "'I think he was killed with magic. The police won't know what to make of it.' Is that accurate?"

Oh my heavenly stars, my phone was still connected to 911 when I was talking to Skylar.

"I, uh, that was… not what I meant." I tried to think of some way to explain away the magic comment.

"Actually, Detective Nakamura, Hayley has a little secret." I stared at her, grateful that she was getting me out of trouble. "She's a witch."

Was she crazy? I kicked her under the table.

"Aieh!" Detective Nakamura shouted. He grabbed his knee.

"Oh no! So sorry, detective." I stood up and nearly lost my balance. I could feel my toes curling. I wanted to run out of the room. "I meant to kick Skylar." Yeah, that was going to help. I wrung my hands and then made myself put them flat on the table. "What Skylar means is that I'm sometimes mean as a witch, but I don't mean to be. It's just that I get afraid and, ah, lash out at people."

He grimaced at me. "So you killed Lucan Gunter?"

"What? Good heavens, no. I don't mean lash out like that. I mean verbally." I shook my head. "Never physically."

We looked at each other.

"Except for that one kick just then," I said. "Let me get some ice to put on that."

I went to the freezer and pulled out a bag of frozen peas.

"She does have quite a kick," Skylar said. "She plays soccer on a local pub team. How about putting your foot up on a chair?" She pulled a chair around for him.

Kneeling by his leg, I put the peas on his knee.

"As long as I'm going to be here for a few more minutes, I wonder if you could tell me if you've ever seen anything like this." He pulled another plastic bag out of his pocket and handed it to me. This one contained a leather thong with a stone disk on it. The disk was elongated into an oval about a quarter of an inch thick and small enough to snug easily into my palm. It had a couple of glyphs carved into its green and black surface. My heart nearly stopped when I saw it.

"Where did you get this?" I asked. "Where did it come from?"

"It was around Lucan Gunter's neck. You seem to know something about this."

"I think my mother might have had a stone like this. When I was a girl. That's all. It was a long time ago."

"Could you ask her about it?"

"I haven't seen my mother since I was five years old."

"Oh. I'm sorry. If you think of some relative who might know about it, please let me know." He reached out his hand to take back the stone disk.

I held onto it. "Can I take it out of the plastic bag?"

"That would make my forensics team unhappy."

I placed the disk in his palm and watched it disappear into his pocket.

The detective stood up then and tried putting weight on his knee. He winced but walked around the kitchen. "Thank you ladies," he almost gasped. He looked at Skylar. "Thank you for the delicious scone. I'm sure you will see my wife in your café in the near future."

"Speaking of which," she said, "when can we re-open?"

"We're still searching the nursery for Lucan Gunter's keys. We should finish today. So you can probably re-open tomorrow."

Skylar showed him out. I stood in the quiet kitchen. I took out the stone disk I wore around my neck and held it between my fingers.

When I was five years old, they told me my mother was gone and would not come back. I went into the closet in my mother's room and closed the door. I sat in the empty dark for a long time. At the back of the closet, my hand fell on this stone disk. As I held it, the stone remembered her. I could feel her in it. Since that day, this stone disk has been the only thing of my mother's I have ever known.

When Skylar returned after helping Detective Nakamura hobble to his car, she looked at the stone in my hands.

"Is it similar?" she asked.

"Identical," I said.

"So the stone disk that belonged to your mother is a perfect match for the one Detective Nakamura has in his pocket."

"And the one he has in his pocket was around the neck of a man who was murdered 50 yards that way." I nodded toward the nursery.

As we were thinking about how scary that connection was, we heard the front door bang open. Somebody was in the house.

"I locked the door when I came back in," Skylar whispered.

Why hadn't we finished that defensive spell we'd talked about?

"Sweet stuff?" a voice called from the front door.

It was my boyfriend, Sanford, back from a sales meeting in Shanghai. In all the craziness, I'd forgotten he was coming back today.

"What's with the news types out front?" he asked when I got to the front door.

Poking my head out the door, I saw that we still had a few reporters and one camera crew in the street. I also saw that a rental truck was backed up into the driveway. A couple of cardboard boxes were sitting on the floor inside the front door.

"What's all this?" I asked, gesturing at the boxes and the truck.

"My stuff. Didn't you get my email?"

I shook my head. Had not thought to check email.

"Well, the funniest thing happened in Shanghai. But why are those people out front?"

I filled him in on the murder. That is, I told him what was known by the general public. I'd never told him I was a witch, so I left out the magic bits.

Sanford was appalled at the whole business. He asked for the fourth time whether I was okay. Then he said, "Don't worry, I'm here to protect you now."

"Which brings us back to your stuff," I said. "And the funniest thing that happened in Shanghai?"

"Right! We were in a meeting with a big Chinese company, negotiating a deal for selling their line of 'intelligent' video surveillance systems. They were offering us huge discounts. One of the Chinese execs suggested that we come up with a slogan for launching these products in the US. These guys feel like they really accomplish something if they come up with a snappy slogan. So I suggest, 'Save Big on Big Brother.'"

"And they fired you for that."

His face fell. "How did you know?"

"Wild guess. What I don't understand is why you're so happy about it."

"Don't you see? They fired me for being funny! When I apply for the comedy writing job in Burbank, this will look great on my resume. It's perfect." He held his hands out and inclined his head in the international gesture of *Don't you think I'm clever?*

"You are clever," I told him. I would have told him he was funny, but I wasn't in a funny mood. "And I'm supposed to store your stuff?"

"Me! You can store me." He held his hands out again, only this time he had the good sense to look a little sheepish. "I can't afford my apartment now, so I thought I'd move in with you. Like we talked about."

I'd been practically tapping my foot, impatient for him to get to this punch line so I could say NO. A big argument followed. He did most of the arguing, if these count as arguments:

- You're not very supportive of my career change.
- We've talked about this many times.
- I love you. I thought you loved me.
- You always just think of yourself.

That last one almost made me change my mind. (Totally kidding.) He did convince me of this: He was just thinking of himself.

At the end of the argument, he gave up and left with his stuff. When I'd calmed down, I cried. I had been kind of in love with him, kind of. I think I cried about everything that was going on. He was just the latest bit of chaos. So much was wrong at the moment.

For instance: Skylar outing me to Detective Nakamura. What had she been thinking?

Furious in a weepy sort of way, I stormed down the hall to Skylar's bedroom. "How could you possibly tell Detective Nakamura I'm a witch?"

"Sorry, sorry. Didn't mean to upset you. It's a trick I learned from Mother. When someone starts snooping into her magical business, she tells them she's a witch. They immediately think she's a whack job and quit snooping for fear they'll get some on them."

Did that make any sense at all? "Never do that again," I told her and went to my room to change into running shorts. In the backyard, I put a ladder against the wooden fence we share with our neighbor, Georgina Clark-Whyte, known by everyone in the neighborhood as the Great Whyte Snark.

I climbed the ladder, balanced on the upper 2x4 of the fence, and stepped onto the roof of Georgina's shed. From there I slid to the ground. I played with her lonely pit bull for a few minutes and then let myself out the gate at the side of her house. I ran toward the beach, looking back at the end of the block to verify that the reporters were still waiting in front of my house. Only three left, and no camera crew.

Over the half mile to the beach, I got into the rhythm of running. I went north on the beach trail, toward the pier. As I dodged around joggers and strollers, I pretended I was running forward in a soccer match. After passing the little marina and the big marina in Redondo Beach, I ran to the end of the Hermosa Beach pier and leaned against the railing, panting, looking out across the Pacific, wondering if my life was coming apart.

Worse than that, was my life caught up in somebody's scheme? Did this scheme start with my mother? What had happened to her? My father would never say more than, "She is gone. She is not coming back. You must let her go."

My own flimsy memories of her were all but gone. Only the recollections in her stone disk kept the memories alive. Standing on the wave-battered pier, I held that stone and felt the traces of her swirl up in me like a rising tide. I didn't know what my mother looked like. I only knew what she felt like.

I closed my eyes. I stopped feeling the wind and hearing the gulls. I only felt the lingering resonance of her passing.

By the time I ran back down the beach and past the last two reporters in front of my house, I was done with worrying and being angry. My boyfriend before Sanford once told me I was dogged in everything but fear and anger. I'm no good at holding onto those agitations. I could move on. I could deal with the situation.

When I unlocked the front door, Skylar was casting a dusting spell on the living room. She apologized again for telling Detective Nakamura I was a witch. I told her to forget that. We needed to take action. First, put a defensive spell on the house, and second, get the invisibility spell to work.

"That's a tall order," she said, holding her cloth out to suck up the dust flying off a bookcase. "We lack a couple of ingredients if we're going to work a good vegan invisibility spell. What's the hurry?"

"I need to sneak into the police station to talk to the stone disk that Detective Nakamura has in his little plastic bag."

"You think the stone knows something important?" she asked.

"The power of it came right through the plastic. That stone is jammed with history. It was pulsing around and around in a loop. And as long as I'm sneaking stuff out of the police station, I want to get back my Tannis Beltane."

"When he let me smell it, I recharged the plant."

"Saw you sneak your finger into the bag. Well played. Oh, also we need to come up with a balm for that pool of melted rock in the herb garden. Maybe I can talk with that rock if we calm it down."

"Mother suggests white willow bark."

"Aspirin?"

"She says use the natural stuff from the tree, not the stuff in an aspirin tablet. In any case, it's magic, so you never know."

Chapter 5

We re-opened the Origins Café and Nursery the next day. The place was mobbed. We sold out of plant stakes in the first hour. The café had a line of people waiting to get in until noon, when Skylar ran out of food. Lots of people bought plants. We tried to smile when they told us how much fun it was to have a plum tree or an azalea from the place where the vampire was killed.

Reporters stuck microphones in our faces. How many times did I say, "I don't know anything about vampires"? One idiot asked if the whole episode was a publicity stunt. I wanted to say, "You're asking if we killed a guy to get publicity for our business?" I restrained myself (barely).

After we closed early for the day, Skylar and I talked about staying closed for a while. We couldn't afford to do that, so we decided that if we had to have this publicity, we might as well surf it as far as the wave would go. Skylar put in orders for more food from her suppliers and called our school friends to get extra help in the café. The former owner of the nursery, Jade, promised to help with plants. I found a fast-turn clothing company online and ordered a zillion T-shirts and baseball caps that said:

Origins Café & Nursery
An Opening in the Forest

I resisted the urge to add "Death to vampires."

On the evening news, I watched myself wear a fake smile and say, "I don't know anything about vampires." I cringed. I'd never be a TV personality.

Skylar said, "You're so cute until you put on a fake smile."

We also learned from the news that the police had arrested Johnny Walen, the plant delivery guy, and charged him with murder. A reporter said that splinters in Johnny's hands matched the wood of the plant stake that killed Lucan Gunter. Now Johnny was famous as "the Van Helsing of the so-called vampire murder."

After tossing in bed half the night, I woke at first light. Just when you need a good night's rest, sleep goes on holiday. Skylar was in the kitchen with a cup of coffee. I took a gulp from her cup. "Let's go to the nursery," I told her. "I have an idea that might help Johnny."

This dawning June day in Redondo Beach was more perfect than usual. The overcast was staying out over the Pacific, and we could see the sun coming up over the San Gabriel Mountains to the east.

In the nursery, I asked Skylar to check the pallets that Johnny had brought in. She "talked" to the wood. Then, we found a plant stake that was holding up a vine in a pot — possibly the last stake left in the nursery. Skylar talked to it and confirmed it was the same wood.

I called Detective Nakamura and left a message that we got our plant stakes from the same company that Johnny worked for, so the pallets he handled might be made of the same stuff. That might be why the splinters in his hands matched the wood of the stake that killed Lucan Gunter.

"Surely they have more on Johnny than matching splinters," Skylar said.

"Maybe Detective Nakamura will call back and explain why he thinks Johnny is the perp."

"*Some*how I doubt it," Skylar said. "But if he does, he'll be impressed at the way you toss around cop talk."

"You mean like 'perp'? Everybody knows the bad guys are perps. You hear it on TV all the time. Besides Detective Nakamura used it in our kitchen."

"Right! That was just before you kneecapped him under the table. If he talks to you at all, he'll be staying out of range of your foot."

"I feel terrible about that. He actually seems like a decent guy. Didn't expect that in a detective."

While we were in the nursery with no people around, we went back to the herb garden to look at it in the light. We found Jade there, sitting on a crate. She liked to visit the nursery for old times' sake, so we let her keep her own key to the front gate.

This had been her family's business since the 1950s until my father bought the nursery for me. After watching me bounce in and out of college for years, he figured I'd never manage to graduate. When I suggested the nursery, he offered Jade a sum that covered her debts with enough left over to buy a nearby condo.

I was about to call her name and say good morning, but stopped. Skylar and I had been talking, but Jade hadn't looked up as we approached. She seemed lost in thought, off in another world. Skylar and I looked at each other.

Jade was a flower child of the 1960s who was a little vague around the edges. But she was engaging and affectionate. You couldn't have a conversation with her without realizing at some point that her hand had been resting on your arm for the past couple of minutes.

Now she seemed lost. While we watched, she reached up and moved her open hand in a circle in the air, as though she were wiping fog from a mirror.

"Jade," I said softly.

She turned her head slowly and looked at me. "Yes?"

"Are you okay?" Skylar asked.

She looked as if she were thinking about it. Then, her eyes drifted up to look at a distant space far away over our heads. "What happened to the Buddha?"

"The Buddha?" I said. "You mean long ago?"

"He was here," she said. "Now he's gone."

"Jade, did you have 'shrooms for breakfast?" From time to time, Jade ate magic mushrooms to send herself into "the ecstatic realm," as she put it.

But she shook her head. "Long ago on other mornings, I sat here next to the Buddha and felt at peace. I've been sitting here alone this morning and find no peace." She put her hand on the little wooden platform next to her.

"The Buddha's gone!" I said.

"Oh, don't *you* start," Skylar said.

I was about to say that someone must have taken it, when I realized where it went. I walked to the vaguely round lump of melted stone and poked it with my toe. "I think this is the stone Buddha that used to sit on that platform over there."

"Oh, I remember that Buddha," Skylar said. "Solid granite. Must have weighed 50 pounds."

"The shipping info on the Buddha will tell us exactly how much it weighed," I said. "Think you can get that lump of rock on a scale? I can't touch it myself."

Skylar was about to lift the stone when Saffron, our orange cat, crept up and sat on it. The cat looked at Skylar in that catty way of saying "This is mine." Then, Saffron began licking her paw and cleaning her face.

Skylar picked up the cat and plopped her in Jade's lap, saying, "Here. You like cats." Skylar squatted and lifted the rock onto its edge. She rolled it down the walkway. "We'll put it on the bathroom scale at home. Jade, why don't you come have breakfast with us?"

Jade stood up, letting the cat drop to the ground without paying the least bit of attention to her. Now that Jade was standing, I could see she was wearing a white dress that was striking with her long red hair. She was inclined to wear flowy clothing. This was the flowiest yet.

While Skylar and Jade were making their slow way out of the nursery, I went to the computer in my office and searched inventory records for the Buddha. I'd bought it a while back, but it was easy to find. Shipping weight, 42 pounds.

When we got the stone lump onto the bathroom scales, it weighed 42 pounds.

"What do we know from that?" Skylar asked. She was making scrambled tofu for breakfast.

"We know we need to think about it," I said, nodding toward Jade, who was sitting at the kitchen table with a cup of chamomile tea. We couldn't talk about the melted Buddha magic in front of her.

"So Jade," I said, "we haven't seen you in a couple of weeks. Watcha been doing?"

"Wandering," she said matter-of-factly.

"How's Bryce?" He was her boyfriend, a landscaper who had worked in the area for many years.

Jade looked perplexed. "He's been acting strangely."

Takes one to know one. "How do you mean?"

"He commands me to wear white. No." She frowned and looked down. Then up. She waved her hand in the air as if wiping off a dirty pane of glass. "No, that was the other man."

She ran her fingers through her long red hair and stared at a strand across her palm. "When we make love, he possesses me completely. Well, both of them." She looked up at me with light in her eyes, suddenly sure of what she was saying: "The men are lordly."

This free love 60s thing was — What's the term? — far out. So Bryce is into domination? And she's got more than one man? Time to change the subject.

But Skylar wanted the racy details. "You're polyamorous these days?"

"Bryce is everything to me." Her brow furrowed. "But the other is… majestic. He instigates the most astonishing activations."

"What exactly does he do?" she asked.

Jade waved her hand as though the answer was obvious. "He penetrates my soul and undoes me."

Skylar and I glanced at each other. That was not the kind of answer either of us was expecting. I changed the subject after all.

"We've been a little undone ourselves lately with the murder. Bad business."

"Yes, Bryce helped identify that fellow who did it."

"Bryce did? What fellow?"

"Johnny Walen, the plant man. Bryce told the police about Johnny's running battle with Lucan Gunter and how Johnny threatened him on multiple occasions. Bryce saw Johnny selling plants at the farmer's market that obviously fell off a truck. In fact, some of the plants were supposed to be delivered to you because they had Origins tags on them."

"Johnny's been stealing from me?"

"Bryce found out. He should have told you. He saw Lucan confront Johnny about it, so Bryce thought Johnny would stop. Instead, it appears that Johnny stopped Lucan."

When we finished breakfast, Skylar walked Jade home. I cleaned up and marveled at how weird everything was. We found out more about what was going on, but instead of clarifying the situation, it seemed more outlandish. Everybody was behaving in ways that made no sense. Jade was stranger than usual, and why would Lucan Gunter object to Johnny Walen's theft of plants? Lucan had nothing to do with our plants — except that right before he'd been killed, he was putting herbs in his pocket.

Skylar came back shaking her head. "Jade is out there."

"She's always been out there. Now she's gone around the far side of out there."

"With an oddly formal way of talking. She doesn't sound like herself. What do you make of that story about Johnny?" she asked me.

"I wouldn't put it past him. The thieving, that is. He is a jerk. Still can't see him killing anybody."

"And melting that stone Buddha?"

"Based on the "no free lunch" rule of magic you've told me about, melting that Buddha would take a lot of magical energy."

"You are correct," Skylar confirmed.

"Who has that kind of power to throw around?"

"Nobody I know. Certainly not Johnny Walen."

"How about Bryce? Have you ever thought that he has magic?"

"Never. Yet he does seem to be leading Jade around on a new leash."

"We should have a chat with Bryce to see if he's behaving as oddly as Jade. Maybe the magical perp cast a spell on them. Are we looking for somebody who's, like, seething with magical power? How can you tell a person has power to burn? So to speak."

"I don't think it's necessarily obvious. Mother has talked a lot about this. She thinks magical people get a feeling when they're around another magical person."

"The way you did with me."

"Right. I'd had that feeling about you for a long time, but until I saw you actually doing magic, I couldn't be sure."

"So we need to catch the perp doing something magical. That might not be easy."

"Especially because magical powers can be ridiculous. When Mother was a teenager, she fell in love with a sorcerer whose toothpaste tube never ran out of toothpaste."

"Um, is that a euphemism for something?"

"You know I asked! Mother would only repeat that it was his magical power. She said he was a little sensitive about it."

"So witches and sorcerers have one basic magical power, and his was a bottomless tube of toothpaste? Poor guy."

"It made Mother realize how difficult it is to spot a magical person. She's worked for a long time to come up with an easy way to detect magical power."

"Could you ask her to step up the schedule on that research project? It might give us the insight we need to spot the killer. And keep ourselves from getting whacked."

Chapter 6

An hour later at the nursery, I looked up and saw a man who was seething with… some kind of magic. I was running a credit card for a woman at the front desk who was buying two pots of succulents. The man locked eyes with me for one second as he walked into the nursery. He didn't smile. He didn't nod. He strode into my nursery as though he owned it. I watched his retreating back until he passed behind a rack of pruning shears.

"Another vampire?"

I looked at the woman standing in front of me. "Beg your pardon?"

"That man," she said. "Dressed all in black. And that ruby stud in his ear. Do you think he's another vampire? Or just a movie star? Though I didn't recognize him."

She leaned closer and whispered to me, "I thought I saw a vampire last week in Anaheim. He looked at me the way that man just looked at you. Made my pulse race, I don't mind telling you. Are you all right? Should we call the police?"

"Yes, yes. I mean, no! Don't call the police. I'm all right. Everything's all right. Let me just check on the, ah, delphiniums." I started in the direction the man had gone.

"Miss!"

"What?" I asked, turning back around.

"My credit card. Could I get it back, please?"

I looked at my hand. I was still holding the woman's card. Fortunately, one of my regular employees was passing. I grabbed her sleeve, handed her the credit card, and pointed at the woman and her succulents.

But before I could get away, a man shouted, "Ms. West! A few boxes for you today."

It was our FedEx guy pushing a hand truck with four big boxes on it. The Origins T-shirts had arrived just in time to frustrate the hell out of me. I took a deep breath and pointed to an area in the corner behind the front desk. "Just dump them there. You need a signature?"

"As soon as I get them all in here," he said, off-loading the stack of boxes. "Only take a minute."

Three stacks of boxes later, he got the signature, and I headed into the nursery looking for the man in black. Up and down I went between the rows of plants. The man was nowhere to be seen. I went into the café and found Skylar in the kitchen sautéing veggies in a pan.

"Did you see a man dressed all in black come in the café? With a ruby stud in his ear?"

She stopped shaking the pan with the veggies and splashed something out of a bottle into another pan. Without looking at me, she yelled, "Nope!" She ran to the prep table, grabbed a bowl of greens, and threw them into a wok. She plated the sautéed veggies on a mound of black rice, stirred the greens in the wok, and dumped the greens on top of the veggies, followed by a handful of pecans. She carried the plate to the pick-up area shouting, "28!"

Leaving the kitchen, I went out to the parking area in front of the nursery just in time to see the man in black get in an old green Buick and drive away. I ran to the front desk and asked the employee I'd left in charge if the man in black had bought anything.

"Yes," she said. "He bought an expensive herb. I had to get Ginger to identify it." Ginger was my assistant who knew about all the plants.

"What was it?"

"Something in the tannis family." She clicked on the computer a few times and said, "Tannis Beltane."

Stepping in front of her, I grabbed the mouse out of her hand. I clicked through to the payments page and entered my password. His credit card record came up: Killin Bardis. His name was Killin.

"No way," I muttered.

"Something wrong?" my employee asked.

I ran to the café kitchen, where Skylar was working with a sauté pan in each hand. I put my mouth next to her ear and said as clearly as I could, "The man in black bought Tannis Beltane."

She stopped shaking the pans and stared at me.

"His name is Killin Bardis."

"No way."

I mouthed "Way" without saying it out loud.

"Killin," she said.

"Killin," I said. I pointed at the cooktop. "Shake your pans."

She grabbed a spatula and moved the contents of the pans around. "Is this Killin still in the building?"

"I saw him drive away."

"If he comes back, call the police."

"Yeah. I'll tell them he's a vampire."

She didn't even look up. The vampire thing was not funny.

We made it through the day. The café's food supply held out through lunch. We sold dozens of shirts and caps and plants. We raked in the money. We were exhausted.

Sitting in front of the TV with the sound off, Skylar and I had frozen pizza for supper (soy cheese). I repeated what I knew about Killin Bardis (his Tannis Beltane purchase, his ruby stud, his old Buick). I told her that the car had surprised me because he looked like the kind of man who would drive something flashier.

"A guy with a ruby stud in his ear would look odd in a beat-up Buick. How old is he?"

"Looked to be about our age. He walks with a little swagger, but not like a thug. It's almost like a ballet dancer swagger, if you can imagine that. He's tall and has chiseled features, a stubbly beard. His hair was spilling over his ears."

"Like that guy?" She was pointing at the TV.

The news anchor had a picture of Killin behind her. I grabbed the remote and shifted the DVR into reverse. From the beginning of the newscast, we heard the anchor say "The police are looking for this man in connection with the so-called vampire murder in Redondo Beach. He is identified as Killin Bardis, 32 years old, and anyone seeing him is requested to contact police immediately. The slain man's girlfriend, actress Melanie Gosford, released these images from a video surveillance camera showing Bardis coming to the front door of the victim's home two days before the murder and apparently provoking an argument."

We saw a broad image of a huge front lawn. Then, the camera zoomed in on a man walking up the curving driveway. It was Killin Bardis.

Skylar said, "How can this be surveillance footage when it zooms in on the guy? This is so fake!"

"Now, now. High-end surveillance systems sense motion and zoom in on whatever's moving. Ex-bf told me about this. We need this for the nursery. And the house."

The video now showed Killin walking up a broad walkway connected to the driveway, presumably to the front door, and pressing the doorbell. The video had no sound, but it was clear that Killin was angry at the person who answered the door, pointing his finger and spitting out whatever he was saying. After Killin's first round of finger pointing, the man he was yelling at stepped out of the door, and we saw Lucan Gunter alive. It was eerie seeing the soon-to-be-dead man in profile, waving his hand dismissively at Killin. Lucan must have gone back inside and closed the door in

Killin's face. Killin stood there fuming, his fists clenched. Then, he turned and walked away. The video ended. The news anchor said that Killin's car was seen in the area of the nursery at the time of the murder.

I called Detective Nakamura and left a message asking if I could come by and see him. It would have been easy to tell him everything in a phone message. I could have said that Killin Bardis had visited the nursery and bought the same type of herb Lucan Gunter had in his pocket when he was killed. But I wanted to find out where the detective's office was so I'd know where I was going when I snuck into the police station.

"If this guy is the killer, why would he come back to the nursery and buy the Tannis Beltane?" Skylar asked.

"Maybe he figured the police were going to be on to him anyway. And what if he was here the first time to get the Tannis Beltane? What if he found Lucan Gunter putting it in his pocket, and that led to the murder?"

"Which raises the question: How did both men know that Tannis Beltane is so special?"

"And is it a lot more special than we know?"

We munched on our pizza, watching the news with the sound off. We watched reports of an apartment fire in Pomona, and shootings in Long Beach and Thousand Oaks. A new elementary school opened in Santa Monica.

"I'm wondering about the way you know that a person is magical," I said. "When Killin walked into the nursery, he looked at me for one second, and I knew instantly he was different. I could feel it so strongly." I put down my pizza and placed my hands on my belly. "It was like an electric current shot through my body. My pulse raced."

"I know that feeling," Skylar said.

"It's so dramatic. Doesn't that make it clear that this person is magical? It's not really such a mystery."

"Well, the world has many kinds of magic."

"Okay, you've told me about the earth, air, fire, and water magic. Those feel different in different people?"

"That's not what I mean. Think about this: You felt this electric current in your gut when Killin looked at you, right? Now I'm looking at you. You know I'm magical. Do you feel that current?"

"Of course not. You're a… girl."

"I think you're catching on."

"I do not feel an attraction to that man!"

"Let me tell you a secret," Skylar said. "Do you remember the first time we met on campus?"

"Only vaguely," I said sheepishly, not really remembering at all.

"Right, well, I remember. You looked at me as you walked by, and I got that electric current in my gut. I started watching you, hoping to see you with other girls, but you were all boys boys boys."

"Oh, Skylar, I didn't know you…"

"It's all right. I got over it. Just one of those little thrills that doesn't pan out. And this one turned out to be good for a different reason. As I watched you, I started to get a different sort of feeling. A little higher than the electric one in your gut that makes you weak in the knees. Up here." She diddled her fingers in front of her forehead.

"One day I saw you sitting on a boulder at the edge of a flower bed with both your hands pressed flat on the rock. I had that feeling in my forehead. I suspected I was seeing some kind of magic. I wasn't sure until that day you talked to the mountain to find the guy who was lost."

I realized I'd been chewing the same bite of pizza for a while. I swallowed. I was struggling to keep myself from apologizing for liking boys. That was a non-starter. But I felt bad for Skylar anyway. And no way was I going to admit I had the hots for Killin Bardis.

"By the way," Skylar said, "Mother always told me that love is the most powerful magic of all. And I'm not interested in males, but Killin Bardis is drop-dead handsome."

"Killin is a bad boy, possibly a murderer. I am not attracted to bad boys. It doesn't make any sense."

She smiled at me. "If it made sense, it wouldn't be magic."

Chapter 7

That night, I had a strange dream. The plot of the dream wasn't strange. It was woman meets man, and they do what women and men have been doing since the dawn of time. I woke up all wet and undone.

What was strange about it was how real it seemed. When I realized I was awake, in fact, I jerked up in bed and looked around the dark room, thinking I would see the man standing there.

After that, I lay awake for more than an hour wondering what this dream was about. Was I already desperately missing my ex-boyfriend? Or was I subconsciously eager to couple with Killin Bardis? Neither explanation pleased me. The second one appalled me.

Eventually, I went back to sleep and woke up two hours later. Once again I found Skylar in the kitchen with a cup of coffee. She looked awful.

"You don't look like you got quite enough sleep," I said.

"I was awake half the night. I had a horrible nightmare."

"So bad you couldn't sleep?" I put water in the kettle to make tea and sat down at the table.

"I had sex with a man!"

"No!"

"I found this man irresistible. Like all of me wanted him, yet all of me felt repelled. I wanted to scream, but no sound came out."

"And this dream seemed vivid? Like it actually happened?"

"Yes!" She began to cry.

"Skylar, I had the same dream." Only I hadn't felt repelled. Mine wasn't a nightmare, not at the time. I was starting to think I was in a nightmare, though. Was this some kind of magic attack? Was someone invading our sleep?

We compared as many details of our dreams as we could remember, which was quite a lot. The details were eerily similar, though not quite identical. One detail was missing for us both: the man's face. In the dream, we had the sense of seeing him clearly. Now his features escaped us.

An hour later, we were heading out of the house and found the front door standing open. I slammed the door closed and locked it.

"You don't think that dream stuff actually happened, do you?" I said, as much to myself as to Skylar. We stood next to the front door for a minute without saying anything, listening. Then we searched the house. Everything was in its place.

Finally, Skylar did what any sensible witch would do in this situation: She called her mother. Skylar put her on speaker.

Her mother thought that someone had ravished us. "It's a perversion of the Great Rite, but it doesn't necessarily mean there was physical contact. It can be more of an intermingling of the spirit. Unfortunately, the ravisher can rend the soul, splitting off parts of you, leaving shadows in the gaps, especially if the person doing it is unskilled or simply doesn't care. I've read that memories can scatter and take refuge in the earth. Sometimes, they're caught by stones nearby. Hayley might be able to sense them."

"So this ravishing is done by a magical person, right?" Skylar asked.

"Yes, so far as I know, only a magical person can do it — usually aided by the power of a magical object."

"Why would someone do this?"

"According to what I've read, it could be a way of controlling someone. The magical person wants power over you. It could also be a way of finding out what you know. The contents of your soul are laid bare."

She gave us a defensive spell that required salt and thyme. It did not call for any icky animal parts. We could do this.

While Skylar got the salt and thyme, I went to my bedroom and picked up a river rock I keep on the nightstand by my bed. I have these stones lying around here and there. When I hold one of them, it calms me. I feel eons of water flowing by from whatever river they came from. The stone next to my bed now had a different story to tell. It had felt the convulsing in the room, the fusing energies. The stone had sensed a physical presence in the room — a man at the foot of the bed.

The hairs stood up on the back of my neck when I "heard" the stone tell how close the man stood. Right at the foot of the bed while I lay there asleep. But I was relieved that he hadn't been any closer. The stone also had a faint impression of the same scene playing out in Skylar's room.

One other bit of knowledge I got from the stone: "Mary Had a Little Lamb." I felt that nursery rhyme rippling in the stone. When I put down the stone, I could recall only that the stone knew a rhyme that I didn't. I should know that rhyme and could feel a rhyme-sized gap where it must once have been. The rhyme in the stone was my memory. Going through life from the age of 31 without "Mary Had a Little Lamb" was not the end of the world, but once I knew of the loss, it was oddly heartbreaking.

Cradling the stone in my hand again, I sensed the rhyme flowing past. This time, I let it flow back to its "home" place in me. I put down the stone on the nightstand and sat looking at it, as "Mary Had a Little Lamb" played in my head. The memory had come back to me.

Sitting on the bed, I wondered how many more times in my life I would think of that little rhyme. Probably only a few times more. Yet, I couldn't imagine myself without it.

I told Skylar that the man had stood at the foot of my bed and her bed. No touchies! I didn't tell her about the rhyme, though it was easy to guess that the ravishing had split off part of her. What memory could she have lost? Something more important than "Mary Had a Little Lamb?" And where might that memory have gone? Until I had some idea where to find it, I wouldn't trouble her with news of a memory whose absence she would know nothing about.

A terrible thought occurred to me then: What if the nursery rhyme wasn't the only memory I'd lost? What if other parts of my past were gone? They could be circling unseen in the stone. How can you recognize a memory you no longer know? A nursery rhyme seems to fit, but what about the sound of a person's voice? The location of something important? The very knowledge that something was ever important at all?

If I could figure out what memories were lost, I could retrieve them from the stone. That was reassuring. Whether Skylar's memories might be in this stone or elsewhere, remained to be seen.

In the meantime, we went out to walk around the house backward. It was still early. The news people weren't camped out front, but a few dog walkers were out. When somebody passed near the yard, we stared at our phones.

"Can't you just see us doing this on the national news," I told Skylar, as we stumbled in reverse over the unmown lawn. "The reporter would say, 'The so-called vampire murder took a bizarre turn this morning when the women who found the body were seen walking around their house backward.'"

"If we look casual about it, no one will even notice. And remember, don't stop walking or we'll have to start over."

I tried to look casual. Here we are, out for a backward stroll. I thought of an outfielder in baseball walking backward, keeping his eye on the ball, casually letting the ball drop into his glove. The pyracantha bush at the corner of the house caught me. Our yard was a little more complicated than a grassy outfield.

"How do we see where we're going and still look casual?"

"Once we get to the backyard, we'll be okay."

We were passing along the side of the house next to Georgina Clark-Whyte's house. I noticed the blinds twitch in her upstairs window.

"Georgina's up," I announced.

"Oh well," Skylar said. "What backward walk would be complete without Georgina?" She smoothly unlatched the gate so we could go into the backyard without stopping.

"What happens with the salt and thyme?"

"Mother said to scatter it on the ground on our third pass."

"And this keeps magical people out of our house? Or all people?"

"Magical people. Those are the only people we're worried about, right?"

"Suppose so. Really I'm uneasy about everybody right now. I don't think Johnny is dangerous, but he was stealing plants. I don't think Bryce is dangerous, but he's doing some kind of domination thing with Jade. And I don't know what to think of Killin Bardis."

We were moving faster now. We went wide around the raised bed where we grew vegetables. Might as well include them in the circle so the magical perp couldn't mess with our green beans.

"Here's a plan," Skylar said. "Next time you see Killin Bardis, invite him over for tea. If he can pass through the circle, he's not magical, so he can't be the perp. Although he can be the other kind of magical. The circle won't keep out sexy lover magic."

"Oh good. If your ex-girlfriend who wore all the chains comes back, she can get in the house, too."

Skylar didn't say anything. We came out the gate on the other side of the house. We walked *casually* backward on our second lap.

"Sorry," I said. "That wasn't nice."

"She was hot."

"Killin is hot," I confessed. "He's just hot wrong. Isn't he?"

"Emmeline with the chains was wrong also. What's a girl to do when hot calls?"

"Killin could be the killer!"

"Whoever the killer is, we have to find him," Skylar said.

"Yeah, it was bad enough that the murder happened in the nursery using magic. But having the killer or whoever it was came in our house last night, that was the last straw," I said, stating the obvious. "He could have killed us. The police aren't going to catch him. If we don't figure out who he is, he'll do something worse. Just protecting the house isn't good enough."

When we came out of the backyard for our third lap, Georgina was standing in our front yard. She was wearing an enormous green shift with giant red hibiscus on it.

"Good morning, Georgina," I said. "You're out early."

"Hayley, what in blazes are you doing?"

Georgina wasn't one to waste time on niceties like good morning. And she didn't approve of the gay thing, so she usually pretended that Skylar didn't exist.

"We're walking backward," I said.

When we passed the front door, Skylar picked up the bowl containing the salt and thyme. She scattered it in our wake. Georgina held back to keep from getting any on her.

"I can see you're walking backward," Georgina snapped. "What's with the stuff in the bowl?"

Skylar said, "We thought as long as we're walking backward, we might as well fertilize the lawn."

"And you're walking backward because?"

"Because we need to fertilize the lawn," Skylar said.

Georgina was following us around the corner of the house. If we didn't give her better answers, we'd have her trailing us the whole way. "We saw it on Good Morning America or maybe that other show. Walking backward is good for your hamstrings."

"Wouldn't it be easier on the sidewalk?"

"It's a balance thing. Broken-field running combined with backward walking."

Georgina rolled her eyes and raised her arms in the air. "Everything's gone off. This vampire business is bad, and I know who did it."

We almost stopped walking at that news. As we slowed, Skylar scattered the salt and thyme to the side so Georgina could catch up. "Who?" Skylar asked.

Georgina rolled her eyes again. "The man's girlfriend, obviously."

Skylar and I exchanged a look. We hadn't considered Lucan Gunter's gf, Melanie Gosford.

"What makes you think she did it?"

"Have you seen her on *The Young and the Restless*? She's got 'killer' written all over her lying face. That woman is a witch."

Chapter 8

That evening, Skylar and I ate our veggie casserole at the kitchen table, avoiding the local news on TV. We were worn out after another long day. We knew we had to keep up with what was going on, but we needed a break, so we were recording the news for later.

For us, the most interesting news was that fewer people were mobbing the café and nursery every day. Our 15 minutes of fame had stretched out to days. Our run in the spotlight might be nearing its end, which would be perfectly okay with us. We only had a few T-shirts left.

"What if she actually is a witch?" I said. "Melanie Gosford."

"I've never gotten that magical feeling when she's in the café," Skylar said. She put down her fork and diddled her fingers in front of her forehead.

"She's a celebrity. What if that creates its own feeling?" I waved my hands in the air like I was going gaga over a movie star.

"I haven't got that feeling, either."

"Really? Not impressed by her work on *Young and Restless*?"

"Oh, yeah, she's good at being bad. You can watch some installments with me if you want. I've got several on the DVR. Melanie's getting a bigger role on the show because she's *so* bad. I love it when she comes into the café, but I don't want to spook her with the star treatment." She waved her hands, doing the gaga thing.

"You're too cool for that?"

"You trying to nail me to something?"

I put my hands on the table and looked Skylar in the eye. "Could Melanie Gosford be a witch?"

"Yes. Happy?"

"If she is a witch," I said, "she could be the killer. Which only makes me happy if we can prove it and get her locked away."

"What about the man who ravished us? That was not Melanie Gosford."

"She could be working with someone." I waved my fork. "Like what if she has a secret conspiracy going with Killin? Or some other man? They needed to get rid of Lucan Gunter, so they did him in?"

"That means we're looking for two perps instead of one. That doesn't really help."

"What if the man who ravished us is really a woman?"

"Hmm," Skylar said. She chewed on the idea. "That would be a diabolical disguise."

"And it might explain why the creep didn't get physical with us when 'he' ravished us."

Skylar got up and pulled a bottle of wine out of the rack in the corner of the kitchen. "That zinfandel we're drinking hates the casserole. How about this merlot? I thought your river rock told you a man was in the room."

"Merlot is fine, and stones pick up physical movements, strong emotions, stuff like that. It's hard to be sure of a person's sex. I assumed the person was a man, based on our dreams."

She popped the cork on the merlot. "You *assumed*. That makes an ass of U and me, according to my father."

"My father said the same thing."

"It's the kind of thing men say that they think is wise." She reached for my wine glass.

I handed over my glass and looked sideways at her. "It is wise."

"Don't encourage them."

She was kidding. Mostly.

"The thing is," Skylar said as she poured the zin into the sink, "whatever's happening with Jade and what happened to us can't be mere coincidence. She said she had *men* possessing her."

"We thought the same thing!"

"Okay. Good point." She put our glasses back on the table. "We could both be wrong. Except that one of *her* men is Bryce. I'm pretty sure Bryce hasn't been going around in drag all these years."

"Is Bryce the perp?"

"If we're looking for a murderer who's magic, Bryce is not the perp." She poured the merlot.

"You don't get that feeling from him?" I diddled my fingers in front of my forehead.

She put down the bottle. "I get a feeling from him, but it's not..." She diddled her fingers.

"What kind of feeling do you get?"

"Like he's a *Man* pretending to be civil."

Calling Skylar a militant feminist would be unfair. It's more like she's simply impatient. She's especially impatient with men who seem house-trained but insist on taking over a task she's handling just fine herself or man-splaining something to her that she already understands. "They assume I'm a dumb girl," she says.

Bryce was like that. He was a polite man who was only dimly aware that other people could get by without his help.

"Even if Bryce is just pretending to be civil, he doesn't seem like a murderer." I sipped the merlot. Much better. "On the other hand, if Bryce happened to walk by while *you* were murdering somebody, he'd probably say, 'Here, let me do that for you.'"

"That sounds like something I'd say," Skylar pointed out. "Are you getting a bit leery of men?"

Rubbing the back of my neck, I admitted that there was a lot to be leery of these days. "I want to talk to Bryce," I told her. "Find out if he seems odd in any way. But I don't think he's the one ravishing Jade. We do think Jade's been ravished like us, right?"

"We do suspect that," Skylar agreed.

"That's scary in every way. She really seemed out there. Could ravishing damage a person that much? Do I seem as scattered as she did?"

"Some days."

"Ha-ha," I pretend-laughed. "That sounds like something *I'd* say."

We'd finished the casserole. I cleared away the dishes while Skylar sat at the table and fretted. I gave her a peanut butter cookie.

"Thanks," she said. She took a bite of the cookie. "That makes everything better."

I sat back down at the table with my own cookie. "Surely the killer and the person doing all this ravishing is the same person."

"If we're willing to assume."

"And surely the most likely perp is Killin Bardis."

"Not Melanie Gosford?" Skylar did the diddly finger thing followed by the going-gaga thing. A few cookie crumbs bounced across the table toward me. "Girlfriend of the victim and evil schemer on *The Young and the Restless*?"

"We should not assume she's *not* the perp just because it seems ridiculous."

"Granted. This whole thing is ridiculous. We should check out Melanie Gosford. In the meantime, did you talk to Detective Nakamura about Killin showing up at the nursery?" She popped the last bite of cookie into her mouth.

"Yeah, he called me back after he got my message and wanted me to tell him about Killin over the phone, but I insisted on seeing him at the police station. I had to get all emotional so he'd think I needed a face-to-face. At the police station, I told him Killin went straight for the Tannis Beltane and bought it without asking for help. Since it was unlabeled, he knew exactly what he was looking for."

"Did you ask the good detective why he's interested in Killin?"

"I did, but he wouldn't tell me anything. Detective Nakamura is all take and no give."

"We need some way to find out what he knows. To begin with, why did he start looking for Killin? I'm guessing it wasn't because Detective Nakamura thinks Killin is hot." She did a swoony version of the going-gaga thing.

Okay, she was getting me back for my comment about her hot ex-gf Emmeline. Ignoring that, I said, "If we could find out more about Lucan Gunter, we might get a clue about why someone wanted to kill him."

"Got a single hit when I Googled him. He was some kind of investment banker in downtown LA. You're right. We need to know what Detective Nakamura knows about him."

"And I want to get my hands on that stone disk that was hanging around Lucan Gunter's neck."

"Seriously, you're going to sneak into the police station?"

"If we can get the invisibility spell working, I can do it. Do you have a better idea?"

"Nope," Skylar said. "I do have an idea that the spell we were working on is never going to make you invisible without eye of newt. Since it's a matter of life and death, we might have to man-up and do the newt."

"Before we lower ourselves by manning-up on poor defenseless newts, let's see if your mother has come up with anything new."

Skylar put in a call to our best authority on witch magic. Her mother had collected a number of old books on magic over the years.

It turned out that Skylar's mother had indeed found another invisibility spell. The traditional potion for this one used squishy animal parts, but the story that powered it seemed open to possibilities. One of those possibilities was Tannis Beltane. This was the story:

Once upon a time on Hoy, Orkney, a young ne'er-do-well named Andon Spens was walking on a ridge above the North Sea. It was Beltane, and all about him in rocky crevasses, the tiny yellow flowers of the Tannis Beltane could be seen emerging in the early light. Where clear water tumbled down a rill, Spens reached over to a plant by a pool and plucked a sprig with three flowers on it.

At that moment, he heard an eerie wailing from the direction of the sea. He turned and saw a mermaid splashing in the waves, a comb and looking glass in her hands. As she combed her golden hair, she sang a lament about the time it had taken her to swim from Aberdeen, where her lover had been killed by a sailor with a harpoon. This song was in the secret language of the sea people, but Spens somehow understood its meaning.

He went down an ancient path along the rocky cliff face. He entreated the mermaid to give him her golden hair, for he knew that if it were woven into fabric, it would give him magical powers.

"What will you give me for it?" the mermaid asked.

Spens held out the sprig of Tannis Beltane with the three flowers.

"Such a small offering," the mermaid said, but they both knew that on this day of the year, the Tannis Beltane had power to grant the sea people a wish. She told Spens that if he gave her the Tannis Beltane, she would return the next morning with fabric woven of sea plants that had the same magic as her hair.

Spens clambered down backward into the surging water, fearing for his safety on the barnacled rocks. He handed the sprig of Tannis Beltane to the mermaid. He was careful not to touch her hand, for he knew that any man who touched the skin of a mermaid would join her in the deep.

The mermaid plucked away the three yellow flowers from the green sprig, saying that they were of no use to her. She put the tiny green leaves of the Tannis Beltane in her mouth and disappeared into the sea.

The next morning, Spens went down to the rocky shingle thinking it unlikely that the mermaid would fulfill her side of the bargain. He was surprised to find a beautiful woman with golden hair standing on the rocks.

"I have brought you the magic fabric of sea plants," the woman said, holding out a shimmering green cloud of airy cloth. "And for your trusting heart, I will be your faithful wife if you will have me."

"Why do so many spells call for walking backward?" I wondered.

"Walking forward is so common. Anybody can walk forward. It's safe to say that the universe is not impressed if you walk forward."

"And what's up with the faithful wife thing?"

"That's the part that gets me in these stories. Why has the beautiful mermaid transformed herself into a human woman only to fling herself at the ne'er-do-well?"

"Maybe the ne'er-do-well is hot."

Chapter 9

Tannis Beltane. What's so great about Tannis Beltane?

Dear Lucas Gunter, why did you tuck some into your pocket just before you were killed? Will we ever find out?

Killin Bardis, someday I will ask you why you bought it.

Detective Nakamura, when you asked me what Tannis Beltane is good for, you weren't satisfied with my answer that it cures the common cold. Which it doesn't do, so far as I know.

On the other hand, it might do that. I'm not sure what it does, although it doesn't seem to do anything on its own. If you're a mermaid, however, it might turn you into a beautiful human woman who fancies a hot ne'er-do-well.

We got Tannis Beltane when Skylar and her mother made a pilgrimage to their ancestral home on the island of Mainland, Orkney. Yes, an island named Mainland. The magic in her mother's line is of that island. And when I say ancestral, I mean lots and lots of ancestors ago.

"Listening" to the plants growing in the Ring of Brodgar, Skylar was smacked by the sound of the Tannis Beltane. She said it was like hearing bagpipes playing "Scotland the Brave" while all the other plants were humming quietly to themselves.

She knew the Tannis Beltane was jammed with magic *potential*. That didn't tell us what kind of magic it could be. It was like discovering gasoline before the invention of engines.

Witches before us knew about this plant. We had evidence of that. But did they use it much? When you get the magic you need from eye of newt and toe of frog, why come up with other recipes?

Because it's fun to invent new spells? Because it's exhilarating? It is! It's a total thrill — like jumping off a building with wings on your arms.

You just gotta hope you stick the landing. To avoid hard landings, most witches and sorcerers stick with proven spells.

Skylar and I had two problems with proven spells. First, they're foul. I can't emphasize enough how disgusting most spells are. They need a good story to power them and some kind of *stuff*, usually a mixture of ingredients. Call it a potion. Skylar's mother thinks that magical patterns were purposely set up to be disgusting to keep away the non-magical.

Our second problem: The power of the little squishy creatures is waning. Newts and frogs are in trouble out there, and they don't pack the wallop into potions that they once did.

Oh, and a third problem with proven spells is that they're not easy to come by. The world's witches and sorcerers are not one big happy family. They're not good at the sharing thing. Some are evil and don't want to reveal their powerful spells. On the other hand, well-meaning witches worry that a powerful spell will fall into the wrong hands.

So, spells are passed down from one generation to the next in families. Since I hardly knew my mother at all and my father never said anything about magic, I inherited no spells. I was a magical orphan.

Skylar's mother adopted me. She started me out on a few simple spells — boiling water without heat, dusting without wiping a cloth around, and convincing snails to leave a garden. These are the kinds of spells that families pass down. Handy things, labor-saving devices.

They still require labor, of course. The universe operates on a "No Free Lunch" policy. But it's a lot more fun to dance a little backward jig and grind thyme to a fine dust than to gather firewood to boil water. At least, it was in the days before electric stoves. Electricity is magic, and I mean that literally.

Some of the spells in the old books that Skylar's mother had were more powerful than boiling water and dusting. They were written in antique language, and they were as much puzzles as recipes. Just figuring out what plant they meant when they called for devil's claw could be a challenge. Four different plants go by that name around the world. Use the wrong one and interesting things could happen.

The A-list spells in the witch world were flying and invisibility. Flying spells took a lot of newt, frog, chicken and bat parts. Get something wrong, you fall out of the sky.

Invisibility seemed safer. Even so, would an invisibility spell only work on half my body or for just half an hour? Or would it erase me forever?

My early attempts with tadpoles showed that one invisibility spell worked well for me, aside from making me ill from the disgusting task of disassembling the tadpoles. That spell did not work for Skylar.

That's the other thing about spells: You gotta have the knack for them. It's like singing opera or shooting quarters out of the air with a pistol. Some people can do it. Some people can't. I was determined to do invisibility and other spells. I was not going to go through life knowing I was a witch without driving the witch thing around and seeing where it could go.

Now with Lucan Gunter showing up dead in my herb patch, I had to do what I could to find the perp. Detective Nakamura wasn't going to. I might not live long enough to drive the witch thing very far if I didn't drive it fast enough to find the killer.

We still had a couple of hours of daylight left, so Skylar and I plucked a stem of Tannis Beltane and drove up the coast to a rocky shore. We parked on a cliff overlooking the Pacific next to a couple of teenagers who were making out in an old Jeep with the top off. They sprang apart and straightened their clothes when we crunched into the little gravel parking area.

"Pardon us!" Skylar called as we got out and walked past them to the edge of the cliff.

We walked and clambered along a narrow path across the rocks to a little cove where the waves crashed onto loose boulders. While Skylar recited the story about the mermaid and the ne'er-do-well, I walked backward into a surging wave, gathered a long strand of kelp, and put the Tannis Beltane in my mouth, wondering if it would turn me into a mermaid. I didn't feel anything unusual.

"Your hair is blonde!" Skylar shouted.

I splashed frantically out of the water to check my rear end for scales. Everything seemed okay except I'd scraped my calf on a barnacle. And I was cold. That water is freezing.

"Should have worn a wet suit," I told Skylar. Pulling my hair around, I could see it was "naturally" blonde and six inches longer than it had been. It was lovely, but I was not invisible.

"You look good as a blonde surfer girl," she assured me. "Unfortunately, I'd say you're more visible now than you ever were as a brunette."

"So much for getting the spell to work."

"Maybe you need to get all the way in the water and let me walk backward to give you the Tannis Beltane." She handed me a towel.

"Good idea. Then, we'd both be cold." I dried off as best I could in my shorts and T-shirt. "As part of an invisibility spell, the story doesn't make sense because nobody in the story turns invisible. Am I supposed to be the mermaid or the guy who picks the Tannis Beltane?"

"I'd say the mermaid." She brushed her fingers through my hair. "Very nice color job. Ne'er-do-wells will flock."

"For anybody with blonde ambitions, this would be a first-class spell. Could your mother have misunderstood what the spell is for?"

"Those old books she has are confusing, but not that confusing." As we scrambled back up the cliff face, she added, "We just need to try different ways of using the story. The thing about spells is that they make an odd kind of sense while not making sense, you know?"

"Like a Bugs Bunny cartoon," I said.

"Now, there's some magic for you. Glues my little nephew to the TV."

When we got to the top, the teenagers were joined at the lips and didn't see us until we were crossing in front of their Jeep. We pretended not to see them but were startled by the boy hitting the horn with his elbow when he heard us walking in the gravel. They looked sideways out to sea and then turned directly toward me. Their brows furrowed. They looked at Skylar, then back at me. A brunette had gone down the cliff, and a blonde had come up.

"Magic," Skylar told them with a wink.

I opened the driver-side door and folded the towel on the seat. We got in and drove off.

"I wish you wouldn't do that," I told her.

"Sorry. Forgot. It's just that I've had bad experiences when I *didn't* do that. Did I tell you about the time I used the stepstool spell in a store?"

"No. But your mother taught me that spell. You look left and right and say 'Cady Goodwife struck up Aragon Hill'?"

"That's the one. Lengthens your arm so you can reach something. I was in a kitchen supply store in the mall and wanted a colander that was hanging way up on a rack. I didn't have time to run around looking for something to stand on, so I ran that spell and grabbed the colander. As I was turning to go, I noticed that a woman with wispy grey hair was standing down the aisle watching me. I'm sure I had a startled look on my face that said 'I've just been caught doing magic.' She followed me out of the store, demanding to know how I'd lengthened my arm."

"You're point being that we should not use magic in public?"

"My point being that if we get caught using magic in public we can make a wacky face and say 'Magic!' to put people off. They'll walk away thinking we're just dippy and they didn't really see what they thought they saw. It must be some kind of trick."

I turned onto the Pacific Coast Highway. We rode in silence for a while. Finally I said, "Let's think about the trick to the invisibility spell. The story only has two characters, and neither turns invisible. Pretending to be one of the characters seems like the wrong approach."

"Unless you want to be a blonde."

When she didn't offer any other ideas, I glanced over at her. "Am I the only one who feels compelled to figure out this problem?"

"Sorry — again. Figuring out spells is not something I'm good at. They don't make sense! They're designed to not make sense. The more spells I learn, the less sense they make. And if the invisibility spell resonates with you, then you might be the best one to interpret how it works."

"Really?"

"No, not really. That's an excuse. I feel helpless, so I'm hoping you can come up with something."

After I'd pulled into our driveway and parked in front of the garage, I said, "How about this: The story has another character in it that we can't see because that person is invisible."

As we got out of the car, I could see Skylar's eyes moving around as she ran through the story trying to find the invisible person. Suddenly, she waved at someone behind me, and I turned to see our neighbor Georgina, who started in surprise when she realized that the blonde was me. I waved and curtsied. She shrugged and went back to watering her roses.

In the house, Skylar told me that an invisible character made as much sense as anything, which didn't help because the stories didn't make sense.

"You say that a lot," I complained.

"I'm trying to keep you from getting too logical. Magic is more like a feeling than a thought. It's like a gush of water that tumbles down a hill. You can see the path it takes *after* it flows. Then, you think it makes sense. But figuring where the water will go in advance, that's hard."

"Rocks know something about flowing water. Rocks feel."

"Well, water and feelings are only examples. I just made that up."

"Hmm, yeah. It's all made up, isn't it?" I went to put on dry clothes. By the time I'd dressed again, I'd had an idea. I took off my sweats and put on my smallest bikini. I put on a fleece jacket over that and pulled the sweat pants back on. Skylar was in the living room watching an episode of *Young and Restless*.

"Melanie Gosford isn't in this one so far," she told me without looking up. "She'll show up soon, though. Everybody else is talking about her."

"I'm going to go talk to the rocks," I told Skylar.

She paused the DVR, looked at me, and looked out the window. "But it's just about dark."

"Rocks talk just fine in the dark. And nobody will see me pressing my flesh against them."

She turned off the TV and stood up. "How long will this take?"

"No, no. Stay here. It's better if I'm by myself so I can focus."

"But what if someone is stalking us? What if they follow you?"

"I'll drive a crazy route out of Redondo Beach to throw them off. If I'm not back by midnight, come find me at that place on Palos Verdes where we had the picnic and saw the whales spouting."

Driving around Redondo Beach with my eyes glued to the rear view mirror, I made sure no one was following me. It was hard to tell in the dark. After a few minutes of staring into my rear view and almost rear-ending somebody at a light, I decided it was all paranoia, and headed south.

The Palos Verdes peninsula is a rocky hill that juts out into the Pacific. It's a nice place to live, if you can afford it. Besides the ocean views, it's high enough to be above the LA smog.

Sometimes, I need a place to go where I can talk with the rocks, big rocks. Getting in touch with the earth is calming. People call it "grounding" for good reason. I'd found a spot near the top of Palos Verdes where I could wrap my arms around a rock that connected me to the spine of the peninsula.

I wound through a posh neighborhood until I reached the dirt track that led into the little wilderness of scrub and rocks near the top of the hill. A few minutes later, I stopped at an outcrop of rock that had a commanding view of the Pacific. That view was all dark aside from a couple of twinkling lights moving slowly past on boats.

Sitting down next to a small outcrop of rock, I took out the paper with the mermaid story on it. After reading it by flashlight, I unzipped the fleece jacket and put my arms around the outcrop of rock. I was hoping that would give me enough contact with the rock.

The rock was still warm from the sun. I went ahead and took off the sweat pants. With better contact, I could "hear" better.

As soon as I got my arms and legs around the rock, I felt the rough warmth of the stone and found myself standing in a vaulted chamber. Water dripped around me and a small stream trickled off to my right. The wall to my left was rough, as though it had been hewn out of the living rock, yet the ceiling was built of interlocking pointed arches. The smooth stones arching over my head fit tightly without mortar. The path at my feet was an intricate mosaic of small stones that formed a pattern I couldn't quite grasp.

Nothing remotely like this had ever happened when I talked to rocks. It was utterly strange. Instead of getting impressions from the rocks, I was transported to a different place.

Listening to the sound of water, drops splashing in puddles on the floor, the babble of the stream, I peered into the darkness at the far end of the chamber, wondering why I was not afraid.

"Why didn't you come for me sooner?" a voice behind me asked. It was the voice of a little girl.

I turned. No one was there. At this end of the chamber, tree roots grew through cracks in the vaulting. Water dripped from them onto the floor. At the narrow end of the chamber, gigantic wooden beams framed a door of heavy planks, shut tight.

Far out of the darkness at the other end of the chamber I heard the little girl again. "You could have come. You could have come sooner."

"Who are you?" I called. My voice echoed around the chamber.

"I'm lost. You might have found me if you'd looked." The girl's voice was familiar, but I couldn't place it.

The sound of the stream to my right was louder now, splashing over rocks.

Raising my voice over the noise of the roiling water, I called, "I'll find you now. Will you come with me?"

The stream was swelling into a torrent, though I couldn't see it. Spray hit my legs, and water flowed around my bare feet.

"On the way here, I stood on the sandy shore for a long time alone, trying to remember what will come," the girl called, her voice clear above the roar of the water. "I saw a gigantic clock carved in the cliff face above. The clock was on fire, and climbing down toward me was a man with the head of a bull. I ran away past a stream that tumbled down the rocks and disappeared into the sea."

"Where are you?" I shouted above the water noise.

"You know that the path to the past has fallen into ruin. That way is no longer open — unless you uncover the secret."

I realized that the girl's voice was familiar because it was my own voice. This was my voice when I was five years old.

That was the last thing I remembered before tumbling away in the cascading flood, calling my own name.

Chapter 10

Someone else was calling my name from a long way off. Someone was shaking me, shining a light in my face.

"Hayley! Hayley!" It was Skylar. She was blinding me with a flashlight.

I put my hand up to shield my eyes. "Stop that," I told her.

"Are you okay?"

"Of course I'm okay." I was pretty sure I was okay. I was still wrapped around the outcropping of rock, which had cooled considerably. Cold fog was blowing off the ocean. I groaned and unwrapped my legs from the rock. Skylar zipped up my fleece jacket, and I staggered to her car.

She got in the driver's side and tossed my sweat pants onto my lap. "Honestly, I don't know how you'd get out of these rock socials if I didn't come bust them up," she said. She got the heater going on high.

The clock on her dash said 11:07. "I asked you to give me till midnight."

"Two hours was long enough to be wrapped around a rock in the dark. And you were shouting your own name, so I knew something was wrong."

I told her the whole story and that I'd been calling to myself as a little girl. "I only know what I sounded like at that age because someone made a video of me playing with a dog at a picnic when I was five years old. I found it in my father's office when he was away from home."

"Why do you think you heard your younger self calling to you like that?"

"No idea." I stared at the lighted numbers of the clock on the dash. Then, I looked out into the dark fog. "Actually, I do have one idea. My mother disappeared when I was five. I think the little girl was sort of mistaking me for my mother. However real she was."

Skylar put her hand on my arm. After a moment she said, "So when you wrapped yourself around that rock, you found yourself transported to another place? And this kind of thing never happened before when you talked to rocks?"

"This was totally different. The biggest difference was that I could see things in that chamber. Rocks can't see. They never showed me anything visual before. They gave me feelings of patterns, like where that lost guy was years ago. But never images."

"Sounds like a dream."

"It was dreamlike in some ways. But the rock of the chamber and the feeling of water splashing from the stream were absolutely real."

"I wonder why it happened that way this time. Did you do anything different?"

"The only unusual thing was focusing on the story that drives the invisibility spell before I grabbed the rock. I think the rock understands the spell."

Struggling to get my legs back into my sweats, I thought about what the little girl had said — the voice of the girl. Who knew whether the little girl was real in any way? But what she'd said had given me a clue about disappearing.

With my sweats halfway on, I stopped and turned to Skylar. "I think I know how the invisibility spell works."

# # #

The next morning we drove to the beach and scooped up a bucket of seawater. Back at the nursery, Skylar read the mermaid story out loud. She held a sprig of Tannis Beltane over the bucket of seawater. I opened a bottle of spring water and poured it over the green sprig. The clear water splashed into the seawater. That was the clue the rocks had given me through the voice of the little girl: "I ran away past a stream that tumbled down the rocks and disappeared into the sea."

In the story for the invisibility spell, the clear water tumbling down a rill represented invisibility. That was the odd logic of the magic. That's what I thought, anyway.

Shucking off the running shoe and sock on my right foot, I pulled up the leg of my jeans. I put my bare foot in the bucket of water. Yow, why hadn't I thought to warm up the water? Skylar handed me the sprig of Tannis Beltane. It was the moment of truth.

"Mother says we can probably undo the spell if anything goes wrong," Skylar reassured me.

Great. I put the sprig of Tannis Beltane in my mouth with my right hand. Instantly, my left hand disappeared. My heart thumped in my chest.

"You're invisible!" Skylar shouted, like I hadn't noticed. "Except..." She laughed. "Cute underwear. I love the little purple ribbons."

Looking down, I saw my bra and panties floating in midair. "What's going on?"

"Polyester," Skylar guessed. "Some spells only work on natural stuff. Your underwear must be unnatural. Look, your sneaker is still visible, too. And the zipper of your jeans."

"Can't sneak into the police station like this, can I?"

"Why don't you just strip off and go in the buff?"

"I am not going naked into the police station."

"You're invisible."

"I am not going naked. What if I become visible in there? The spell wears off at some point."

"Look at it this way, if you become visible naked, they'll just think you're a nut job."

I took my foot out of the bucket of water. It was numb from the cold, but I didn't realize that until I stamped it on the concrete floor. Ow. "I don't feel like you're hearing me."

"We could make you a Ninja suit."

"No time for Ninjas. I need to get going. Your mother said this spell lasts three hours?"

"Right! Let's go find some kind of outfit that disappears."

We drove home from the nursery with me lying in the back seat so no one would see my bra floating in midair. As luck would have it, our neighbor Georgina was walking out to get her morning paper when we pulled into the driveway.

"You'll have to shed those clothes before you get out of the car," Skylar told me. I wrestled out of everything in that tight space. More time wasted. I put my T-shirt back on, figuring that was one thing I could wear that would be invisible. 100% cotton.

Skylar waved to Georgina, who acknowledged the greeting by opening her paper and acting like she was reading the headlines. Skylar held the front seat forward and pretended to mess with her phone while I slipped out of the car.

When Skylar looked up from her phone, she said, "Uh uh uh!" She sped up to put herself between me and Georgina. "Your tag is showing," she hissed.

Try to find an article of clothing that does not have a polyester tag on it or polyester thread stitching it together. We ended up cutting the tag out of my T-shirt, including the little nubbin end that was sewn into the edge. Same for an old pair of baggy plaid pants. If I turned visible, I'd have holes in my clothes, which was the least of my worries. Skylar found me an old pair of moccasins — not a vegan solution, but they disappeared when I put them on, so I ran with them (so to speak).

"Say 'ah'," she told me, making a motion with her finger like a tongue depressor. She peering into my mouth. "Yeah, fillings. You need to keep your mouth closed."

I closed my mouth.

"I don't see anything else. The thing is, you're only going to have a couple of hours before you turn visible again. I think we should wait and run this spell another time so you get a longer shot at it."

"The whole thing should only take an hour. If I turn visible, worst case I'll go to Detective Nakamura's office and tell him I walked in with a couple of cops who were flirting with me. He'll lecture me and escort me out. Probably."

"If he catches you with stuff from the evidence room, you'll be in a world of trouble."

"Well, I'll ditch that stuff before I turn myself in, won't I?"

Skylar found a parking space around the corner from the entrance to the Redondo Beach police station. Sitting in the car, we could just see the top of the building behind a white cinder block wall topped with metal spikes.

"It's like going into Mordor," Skylar said.

I didn't laugh. My heart was thumping again. "I'm little Frodo." I scratched my invisible leg with my invisible fingernails and tried desperately to think of another way to solve this problem, to get this killer out of our lives. Desperation wasn't helping my logical thinking. But then I did have a useful thought.

"Wait a minute. This isn't Mordor. This is a little police station in little Redondo Beach. Let's do this."

Skylar came around and opened my door so the people on the sidewalk wouldn't see the door open and close by itself.

"Okay," she whispered, closing the door. "15 minutes."

I ran to the front door of the police station, dodging around to keep from running into anybody on the sidewalk. People were coming and going through the front door every couple of minutes, so it was easy to slip through with one of them. Inside was a front desk manned by a police sergeant, or womaned by a police sergeant today. To the right was a security door that officers used. Mostly officers came and went in their patrol cars or through a back entrance, so I had to wait a few minutes until an officer came out to speak with a person at the front desk. I stuck my foot in the security door as it was swinging shut. Squeezing through quickly, I hoped no one would notice that the door took longer than usual to close.

So what if they did? They wouldn't jump to the conclusion that an invisible girl had just held it open. I relaxed a little. I realized for the first time that I faced a deep philosophical invisibility question: How much could I mess with people?

Passing a burly officer in the hall, I blew on the side of his face. He reached up and scratched his face without looking around.

As I was about to try the same trick on a woman carrying a file folder, she suddenly changed course and bumped into me. I opened my mouth to say, "Sorry" and managed to not say it as she looked around in surprise. Then, she inspected the bottom of her left shoe, shook her head, and walked back the way she'd come.

Finding Detective Nakamura's office was a snap because I'd talked with him there. But as I stood outside the closed door of his office, I wondered if he was actually in there. Did I dare open the door and look? Messing with strangers seemed like fun. Messing with someone I knew felt dangerous. Still, if a door swings open and you don't see anyone, you don't assume the invisible girl did it.

Easing the door open slowly, I peeked in. No detective. Rats. I wanted to search the office to find the police report on the murder, but I only had a few minutes to find Detective Nakamura.

I left the door open and ran down the hall, peering through glass doors into conference rooms. The Redondo Beach police station was not enormously big, so I figured I could cover it quickly. After several minutes of running, I was beginning to wonder if the detective was late to work. A clock on the wall said

9:48. I'd circled through the building and was about to reach his office again when I saw him come out of the men's room. Fortunately, it hadn't occurred to me to look in there.

He had just noticed that the door to his office was open when his phone played the theme to "The Big Bang Theory." It was Skylar calling as we'd arranged, 15 minutes after I left her. She told him that we'd found an uncle of mine who remembered seeing a stone disk like the one that had been around Lucan Gunter's neck when he was killed. The disk my uncle remembered had come from Wales. Skylar asked the detective if he'd noticed that Lucan's disk had a tiny inscription of Cymru, the Welsh name for Wales.

Detective Nakamura hadn't noticed that on the disk in his evidence room. How could he? We'd made the whole thing up. As we'd hoped, he made a bee line for the evidence room. It was a good thing we used this trick because the room didn't have a sign on it saying "Evidence Room." It was labeled "A5."

At the last moment, I tried to dart ahead of Detective Nakamura so I could see the numbers he entered on the keypad next to the door of the evidence room. Fail. Then, I was on the wrong side of him. When he went in, the door nearly slammed shut before I could grab the handle and pull it open again.

He was already striding down the aisle between two high rows of shelves. Hundreds of cardboard boxes, manila envelopes, and plastic bags were piled on the shelves. If Detective Nakamura hadn't been leading me straight to the stone disk, I would've searched all day for it. I felt so clever for thinking up this plan, I could hardly stand it.

The detective stopped in front of a cardboard box that said "Lucan Gunter" on it. Could have found that after all. Detective Nakamura pulled out the plastic bag containing the stone disk and carried it to a small table in the corner of the room. He put the disk under a large magnifying glass on a stand and turned on a light. Sitting down in a chair, he studied the markings on both sides of the disk. Then, he shrugged and carried it back to the cardboard box.

When he'd gone, I took the disk out of the box. I also took out the plastic bag containing the Tannis Beltane. The plant was wilted but might survive if I got it back in the ground soon. Stealing police evidence bothered me. It was wrong. But letting this plant die here in its little plastic bag could hardly do anyone any good. And it would be a crime against magic.

I took the plant out of the bag and slipped it gently into my pants pocket. Out of another pocket I pulled the Tannis Granadus I'd brought with me. This was a far more common member of the Tannis family, not nearly as valuable. I put the Granadus plant in the plastic bag and dropped it into the box.

Over at the little table, I slid the stone disk out of its plastic bag. Once again a thrill passed through me as I saw how similar it was to the one that had belonged to my mother. I sat down in the chair and picked up the disk.

Instantly, it was as if I were in a wind tunnel with plants blowing past me. As they blasted by, I heard their names and their properties spoken so fast I could barely understand what I was hearing. Far in the distance I could see endless streams of plants swirling, gathering into dense masses, flying apart again into separate streams like enormous flocks of green birds. Some of the streams flew around my head before speeding away. Some streams whirled in front of me like green dust devils. As the plants flew around and past me, their rapid-fire descriptions came at me, chittering, squeaking. This went on and on as I sat there, completely fascinated.

Until a noise in the room made me jump.

I dropped the stone disk and turned to see a police officer striding in the door. If I picked up the disk again, I might be lost in it, so I left it on the table.

The officer went to a box at the other end of the room, put something in it, and went back out the door. I sat in the chair, panting. What was I going to do now? The knowledge in the stone disk was incredible. The stone held information about countless plants. I couldn't leave it in the evidence box. It would be lost forever in the Redondo Beach police station. But I had a queasy thought: I was about to leave an empty evidence bag that should have a stone disk in it. That seemed like a really bad idea.

On the other hand, if I took the stone disk, it might help me find the murderer. It certainly seemed like it would help me more than it ever would Detective Nakamura.

As I was worrying about what to do, I noticed a clock on the wall. 11:25. I'd sat at the table holding the stone for more than an hour. I had to get out of there.

I used the plastic bag to pick up the disk and drop it in my pocket.

Then, I pulled off the braided hemp cord hanging around my neck. I looked at the stone disk hanging on it, the stone disk that had belonged to my mother. Using a pair of scissors that were lying on the table, I cut the cord and slid the stone off into my hand. This might be the last time I would ever hold it. The traces of my mother swirled into me.

I had no time for this. Dropping the stone onto the table, I scooped it into the plastic evidence bag. I dropped the bag into the box that said "Lucan Gunter" and went quickly to the door of the room. Two police officers were walking by when I came out into the hallway. Why hadn't I looked? I flattened myself against the wall as they went past. They were talking and didn't even notice that the door to the evidence room had opened and closed again.

Breathing a sigh of relief, I was ready to get out of the police station. But I didn't get very far. My baggy pants were caught in the door.

This was not a huge problem. I could deal with this. I told myself that several times, as I pulled at the invisible fabric. If I had to I could just rip the pants. I told myself that as I tried to rip the fabric. It was tougher than I expected.

Then, I noticed that I could faintly see the plaid pattern of the fabric. I looked higher up and saw a faint flicker of my white T-shirt. My clothes were becoming visible. I had a hunch that all of me would appear shortly.

My worst-case plan was to turn myself in to Detective Nakamura and get him to let me out. Now I realized that Skylar had called him and sent him on a wild goose chase to the evidence room. He would know I was up to something. Would he think I was trying to tamper with evidence that I murdered Lucan Gunter?

Suddenly, my worst-case plan seemed a lot worse than I'd imagined.

Chapter 11

Crap. Crap. Crap. With my pants caught in the door of the police evidence room, I was slowly becoming visible. Anyone who came down the hallway would see my clothes hanging in the air. Even if I got free, it wouldn't do for my baggy pants and T-shirt to be seen walking out on their own. I could strip them off and run out bare-butt, but I was likely to lose my invisibility any time now.

Then, I had an idea. I reached into the pocket where I'd put the Tannis Beltane and plucked a couple of leaves. Maybe it would boost the invisibility spell. Maybe it would give me a little longer. I put the leaves in my mouth.

Living in the plastic bag for several days hadn't improved the taste of the herb. Yuck.

Now I heard two police officers talking, coming in my direction. They were rounding the corner into the hallway where I was caught in the door. My clothes were vaguely visible. I had to make a run for it.

As I was pulling at my pants with all my might, the plaid pattern faded from view. I flattened myself against the wall. The two officers stopped at the door, and one of them went to punch in the security code.

I was standing in front of the keypad. He was about to poke me with his finger.

Leaning sideways, I got out of the way just in time, but when the door opened and freed my pants, I fell on the floor. One of the officers looked down. He looked up. Frowning, he went into the evidence room.

I ran for the exit. By the time I got out to the sidewalk, my pants were becoming visible again. Most of the people passing by were busy with their phones. Nobody seemed to notice the empty T-shirt and baggy pants running down the sidewalk.

Skylar was not parked where I'd left her. I looked around for a place to hide. If I could avoid being seen until I was completely visible, I could walk home. A public park was only a couple of blocks away, but I'd have to cross busy Catalina Avenue to get there. I looked for some bushes I could get behind.

That's when the Girl Scouts spotted me. They were across the street, walking toward the park, when one little brat pointed me out to the woman who seemed to be the troop leader. Then, they were all looking my way. The woman divided them up and sent them across the street in a pincer movement to surround me. How could this be an appropriate activity for young girls?

Before they could get across the street, I dashed in the direction of the park. My clothes were completely visible now. As I ran toward an old woman driving a scooter on the sidewalk, she saw my empty outfit coming at her and screamed.

Dodging a baby carriage, I took a couple of leaves of Tannis Beltane out of my pocket and put them in my mouth, but it didn't help. My body was becoming visible little by little. I could see the fingers of my left hand but not my right.

I reached Catalina Avenue and started across. The light had just changed, and four lanes of cars were starting to move across my path. I changed course and ran south along Catalina. A man in a pickup truck saw me and slammed on his brakes. I guess that's what some people do when they see a partly invisible woman on the sidewalk. The BMW behind him failed to stop in time. The SUV behind the BMW failed to stop in time. I kept running.

A horn was honking on the far side of Catalina. I hoped it didn't have anything to do with me. A siren blared several blocks behind me. Was my face visible now? What if somebody was catching this on video? My life could get very complicated.

At the next intersection, a car turned against the light, honking its horn. It was Skylar. She'd been honking to get my attention for the past block. She pulled up and flung the passenger door open so I could dive in, and we sped away.

Skylar drove a zigzag route through Torrance until we were sure no one was following us. She pulled into the parking lot in front of an upholstery business that wasn't open. We sat there dazed for a minute.

"Are you all right?" she asked.

"Never better."

"You look like a scary mess."

I flipped down the sun visor and looked in the little mirror on the back of it. One eye and my nose were visible. My lower lip was mostly visible.

"This is okay," I told her. "If anybody caught me on video, my face won't be recognizable."

"Good point. By the way, Mother called while I was waiting for you and told me she'd deciphered the word in front of 'three hours' in the invisibility spell. Turns out it's an Old English term for 'approximately.'"

"I kinda figured that out the hard way. And by the way, why weren't you waiting at the spot where I left you?"

"Meter maid chased me off. Said she was going to call the guy who puts boots on cars if I didn't move. When I offered her 40 bucks to leave me alone, she got on her radio and called for backup. I've been driving around the block looking for you ever since, wondering how I was going to find the invisible woman. I'm glad you're okay."

"Thanks. It was fun at first. I got the feeling I could do just about anything without people catching on that an invisible person was around."

"Did you find the police report?"

"No, I had to get to the exit fast when the 'approximately invisible' time ran out. I did get the stone disk that Lucan Gunter had around his neck. It's amazing. It's jam packed with information about herbs."

She stared at me. "So you listened to it while you were in there?"

"When I picked it up, it caught me immediately. Information about plants streamed by me for more than an hour before I got out."

"So Detective Nakamura will never have any idea what he's got in there."

"Well, it's not in there anymore. Frodo has the Precious."

Her eyes went wide. "You took the disk?"

"I had to, didn't I? It might help us solve the murder. I don't think it was going to do anything for Detective Nakamura. And for that matter, what was Lucan Gunter doing with it? Did he have any idea what's in this stone disk? It's like having a whole Internet of arcane plant knowledge in the palm of your hand. Any herbalist would kill for this thing."

Skylar had pulled into our driveway. She shifted the car into park, and we sat there looking at each other.

"Maybe that's exactly what happened," she said. "Only you came along before the killer could take the disk from around Lucan's neck."

I nodded in agreement. "It's a theory."

# # #

That night on the news, we saw my T-shirt and baggy plaid pants running down the sidewalk. Two of the girl scouts had got me on their phones. The news anchors commented that it looked like the scouts were working on their merit badges in movie special effects. "Industrial Light and Magic will be looking for these girls in a few years." Ha-ha.

"It was magic all right," Skylar said.

"And it does seem kind of funny now that it's over," I told her.

The next news item wasn't funny. The body of an herbalist in Yorba Linda had been found in her house. She'd been dead for several days. Police suspected foul play.

We'd met that woman, Deedee Piper. She was a friend of Jade's and a famous herbalist, author of three books on South American plants. We watched video of the police wheeling a body bag out of the house. And there was Detective Nakamura in the background, talking with another man in a rumpled suit.

Skylar turned off the sound, and we watched the weather report for a minute without saying anything. On the screen, an animated sun shot its yellow rays down on the California South Bay.

Finally Skylar said, "Yorba Linda is way out of Detective Nakamura's jurisdiction, so he must believe the two murders are related. Which makes sense. Lucan was obviously interested in herbs, so two herbalists have been killed."

"I thought you found out Lucan Gunter was an investment banker."

"Well, he was also killed in an herb patch with Tannis Beltane in his pocket."

I got up and walked to the window. "What if he was a sorcerer?"

"Yeah, that possibility has been bothering me, too," Skylar said. "He pulled up a magical plant. He had a stone disk that's full of herbal knowledge, but only someone with your magical talent can read it."

Opening the blinds, I looked out and saw our neighbor Georgina on the sidewalk out front with her pit bull. She never walked that dog. In fact, the dog was looking around in disbelief. Georgina was talking with another neighbor. She pointed at our house. I closed the blinds.

"On the other hand," Skylar said, "I'd seen him in the café several times with Melanie Gosford, and I never got the magical feeling about him." She diddled her fingers in front of her forehead.

I paced past the TV and turned it off. "Is it possible Melanie Gosford's *Young and Restless* gaga aura threw off your magic sensor?"

"Not that again," Skylar said. "Yes, I suppose it's possible."

"If Lucan Gunter was magical, that could mean his killer is *not* magical. We could be barking up the wrong tree." I sat down again on the couch and started stacking the coasters on the coffee table.

"We're sure magic was involved in Lucan's murder," Skylar summarized. "But it could be his own magic. At the same time, his killer could also be magic — one magical person taking out another magical person. This could be some kind of battle between sorcerers."

"And this battle just happens to play out in the herb patch of two witches? That's a scary thought." I was relatively new to the witch business. Had I walked into a world that was a lot more dangerous than I'd imagined? Oh, who was I kidding? This had always been the world I'd lived in, the world everybody lived in. We just didn't understand what bad sorcerers and witches could be up to. Were we beginning to understand?

Skylar pulled a couple of different wry faces before she said, "Maybe it's not mere coincidence. Maybe it's all of a piece. Magical people fighting over the turf of magical people."

"But that's terrifying! We're in the middle of a battle and we don't even know? Like some of kind of magical gang war? Have you seen this kind of conflict before?"

"No. It's easy enough to imagine, though. I'll ask Mother about it, but what's important right now, it seems to me, is dealing with what we already know about — two people killed in ways that seem related. How do we figure that out?"

"It would help a lot to know whether Deedee Piper was murdered the same way as Lucan Gunter. If her head was twisted like his, we'd know the killer was magical."

"Or we might still be guessing that everybody involved is magical. In any case, that information should be in the police report that's probably lying at this minute on Detective Nakamura's desk." I got up off the couch and headed for the kitchen. "You want a muffin?"

"Yes, please."

When I came back with the comfort food, we talked about how the nursery and café had gotten along without us for most of the day. They had not gotten along very well. We had good people working for us, but they weren't the best decision makers on their own, especially in the café.

When we'd eaten the muffins and worn out on talking about business, I told Skylar, "I'd like to go back into the police station early, before Detective Nakamura gets in. And this time, we need a backup plan in case something goes wrong with picking me up."

"An out-of-sight rendezvous place would be nice."

"And I need a new outfit in case I become visible in public." I gestured toward the TV. "My plaid pants are now famous. I wish I had a burka."

"What's a burka?"

"You know, one of those cover-all outfits women wear in the Middle East. Like a space suit for earth. If my clothes become visible, nobody could tell that the person inside was invisible."

"I'll make you a mask you can put on if you start to become visible in public. Better yet, make sure you're in a safe place when you become visible! How about that for a plan?"

"I like it! I'll do that."

Chapter 12

The next day we woke up bright and early — half an hour earlier than intended — because the earth shook. The California coast got little earthquakes fairly regularly, and we reminded each other that a little shaking is good. Small earthquakes release tension, reducing the chances that a fault will tear loose in a big way all at once. Also, little earthquakes remind us to put little wads of museum wax on the bottom of anything valuable that might shake off a shelf.

The earthquake that struck that day at 5:21 am was stronger than average, and it shook a couple of items off shelves. It started with a punch and then kept up a rolling shake for 30 seconds or so, which seems like forever when you're standing in a doorway wondering if the house is going to come down around you. It didn't.

We got dressed and went to the nursery to see if anything was damaged over there. Several breakable items had smashed together in the café. I helped Skylar clean up. Being there reminded us of all the stuff we needed to straighten out after being away the day before, so we postponed my second foray into the police station.

Sitting at my desk doing paperwork, I thought of something else I wanted to do. I'd put Lucan Gunter's stone disk in a cloth bag so I could handle it without touching it. If I touched the stone, I'd get lost in it.

I slipped the stone onto my desk and held my hand over it, feeling the pulsing energy. I wanted so much to cradle it in my palm and discover all that it held. I could set a timer on my phone and talk to the stone for a few minutes. That probably wouldn't get me anywhere. In the hour I'd spent with the stone the previous day, I hadn't been able to exert any influence on the sounds and images that raced through me. I needed two or three hours to have a chance at slowing down the flow, to see if I could find specific information. For instance, what did the stone know about Tannis Beltane? I got the stone into the cloth bag without touching it and put it back in my pocket.

An hour later, Skylar yanked open the door of my office and stuck her head in. "Killin Bardis just came into the nursery," she whispered breathlessly.

As we snuck back toward the herb garden, she explained how she'd seen him. "I was going back to pick some thyme and rosemary to put on potatoes for lunch and saw him walking in front of me. I got that feeling." She diddled her fingers in front of her forehead.

"You didn't see his face?"

"I only saw the side of his face, but I'm sure it's him. That swagger. And if it's not Killin, it's some other sorcerer."

"What if he attacks us? Do you have some kind of defense against the dark arts?"

"We could yell 'Stupefy.' Slow him down for a second while he laughs."

We crouch-walked behind a row of potted plum trees and saw him in the herb garden. It was Killin Bardis all right. My tummy fluttered at the sight of those angular features. The ruby stud in one ear. The way he moved. It wasn't really a swagger. More like he was dancing through the world with complete confidence. Was that arrogance?

My musings abruptly ended when I realized that one of the man's confident moves was to uproot my herbs. I wasn't going to put up with that from anybody. I came storming out of the plum trees.

"Hey, you jerk-wad! You can't do that to my plants."

"I was wondering if you'd ever see fit to defend them," he said with the slightest Irish accent, barely glancing in my direction. He continued to pull plants out of the ground and toss them into a little pile.

"It wouldn't be necessary to defend them if idiots like you didn't come in and mess with them."

"You have dangerous plants here. Leaving them undefended is an error."

"So what are you doing? Defending them by pulling them up?"

"My understanding is that these plants are for sale," he said, finally looking directly at me. "I'm choosing plants for purchase."

Hadn't thought of that. I grew some of the herbs in the ground because they didn't do well in pots. To buy them, customers had to dig them up. "Well, you could have asked for help rather than just pulling them up like that."

"I don't require help."

"You need something to put those in," I said, all wrong and indignant. "Let me get you some pots."

"That would be helpful," he said, without a trace of irony, which only made me more angry and embarrassed. "Nothing plastic."

On my way to get some terracotta pots I passed Skylar, who was still standing behind the plum trees. She was holding her phone out between two trees.

"I'm getting everything on video in case there's a problem," she told me.

"Great. If I want to see what a stupid idiot I was, I can watch that later."

I brought back several pots and a bag of potting soil. I squatted next to Killin's pile of plants and began putting them in the pots.

He was looking at a couple of small shrubs at the end of the row of herbs.

"These are goldenseal plants," he said.

"Yes."

"No one has been able to cultivate these," he said, as if he thought I was doing something suspicious. "You don't even have them in a special environment."

"They're in special soil. They're particular about minerals. And the microbiome." I took pride in understanding that last term. It sounded like I was trying to impress him, I realized too late. I didn't tell him that I got the soil right by talking to the minerals or that Skylar talked to the plant to balance the microbiome.

He squatted down next to me and began potting some of the plants he had pulled up. I felt like I was in high school again, sitting next to a boy I liked, hoping our shoulders would touch.

"Are you an herbalist?" I asked him.

"I can't claim that status. I'm collecting information on plants that might be of use in certain ways."

We both stood at the same time and our shoulders touched. I could feel my pulse quicken in my throat. I tried to rub my arm and found that my hand was gripping three pots.

"Look," I said, "I'm sorry I shouted at you."

His dark eyes looked directly into mine. Surely he could see me blushing. "You were defending your plants."

"Right. Yes. Do you think I should put a fence around them?"

"A high fence — a wall — yes. That would reduce the need to control people by force." He turned and said over his shoulder, "Or by shouting at them."

He strode away toward the front desk. I hurried to catch up with him. His long strides carried him at quite a clip, yet he never looked as though he was in a rush. When we got to the front desk, I tallied what he had collected — all arcane herbs that few herbalists would know. I'd learned about most of them from Jade.

After he'd gone, I stood at the front desk nodding slightly in rhythm to some idiotic song that was playing in my head. The song wasn't idiotic at first. It only became idiotic when I realized that Skylar had been standing next to me for a while looking appalled.

"What?" I complained.

"You cannot like that arrogant man. That jerk-wad, as you so elegantly put it."

"I don't like him. And I only called him that because I thought he was messing with the plants. Which turned out to be a mistake on my part."

"He's probably the murderer! Don't you remember he had a confrontation with the murder victim? Didn't you hear what he said about using force to keep people away from the herbs?"

"That's not what he meant. He thinks I should protect the herbs better, and he's right."

"Okay, he *is* right. And he *was* buying plants. And he is still an arrogant jerk-wad. Also, probably a murderer. And you will not be attracted to him, is that clear?"

Some people find Skylar a little pushy. Keeping girlfriends has been a problem. She tends to like outgoing, independent types, but those types of women don't care to be directed by Skylar when she has helpful ideas about what they should or should not be doing.

Having learned to find ways around my domineering father, the super-alpha pack leader, I found Skylar's attempts at herding me unconvincing. It was like having a hamster try to surround me, squeaking that I should go this way or that. The other trait that made Skylar easy to deal with is that she was self-correcting if I just gave her long enough.

Before I said anything on this occasion, she wanted to back-out her instructions: "I didn't mean to say it that way. In fact, I didn't mean to say that at all."

"I see."

She was rocking her head back and forth, but I don't think it was in time to any particular tune, unless there's a song called "Why Do I Say Bad Bossy Things?"

"Really," she said, "you can be attracted to anybody you want. Of course."

"Buuuut?"

"You're not really attracted to him, are you? I mean, you're not blindly going along with whatever he's up to?"

"Not blindly, no."

"Sorry. I didn't mean to say that either. Damn." She stamped her foot. "Anyway, I know you won't put up with anybody who acts like lord of the manor."

"You, for instance?"

She pouted. "That's not fair." She looked away at the wooden bird houses hanging up for sale near the front desk. "All right, it's not *unfair.* I'm just trying to make sure you understand. You don't know how evil sorcerers can be."

"Skylar, your father is a sorcerer. He's not evil. Don't you think it's possible that Killin Bardis is one of the good ones? And isn't it also possible that I could possibly be attracted to him precisely because he's the first magic man my age I've ever met?"

"Ohhhh, I see," she said, rubbing her eyes. "Oh dear. I've been a little slow on this. You've got an idea there's something magical about a relationship between magical people."

"I don't know. This is all so new. It's got me thinking about what my life will be like, being a witch and being with someone who *doesn't* have magic. Do I hide my magic from him? Do I keep that part separate somehow? Do I trust him with the secret, and does that lead to any sort of jealousy? But if I have a relationship with someone magical, everything is possible. I mean, have you thought about that?"

"Yes." She slumped onto the stool behind the counter. "I have thought about that a lot."

A woman walked up with a flat of creeping thyme. Skylar slid off the stool so I could get to the cash register. When the woman had paid and left, Skylar told me that we didn't have any evidence that Killin was dangerous, other than the confrontation with Lucan Gunter, and if I wanted to be friendly with him, she would give him the benefit of the doubt. She walked off toward the café. I got somebody to mind the front desk and went back to my paperwork.

An hour later, Skylar yanked open the door of my office again. This time, she rushed in and locked the door behind her. She turned to face me, out of breath and white as a sheet.

"He's the killer," she hissed. "He's back in the herb garden."

"How do you know it's him? Did you call the police?" I whispered. She shook her head. I reached for my phone, and she put her hand on my arm.

"It's magic, Hayley."

"What's magic? What's going on?"

"Killin! He used magic to kill Lucan Gunter."

"Skylar, Skylar, I thought we agreed to give him the benefit of the doubt."

She didn't answer. Why was she being like this? Was she jealous of Killin? The idea that I might be attracted to another magical person and a man at that, was that threatening to Skylar?

She dragged a chair around to my side of the desk and sat down, messing with her phone.

"So are we calling the police?" I asked her.

Still no answer. Finally, she held her phone up where we could both see it and pressed play. Greenery flashed by followed by the russet leaves of the ornamental plum trees. The leaves parted and I could see Killin in the herb garden, pulling up plants. Then, I saw myself confronting him, yelling "Hey, you jerk-wad!"

Skylar swore and messed with her phone. "This one," she said.

Again I saw the leaves of the plum trees and Killin in the herb garden. He wasn't pulling up plants. He had an odd-looking contraption with two handles and a round knob on top. The device had a metal point on the bottom, several inches long, so the whole thing looked like an oversized dagger with a ball where the hilt should have been. Holding the two handles, he thrust the point into the ground next to the goldenseal bush. Then, he folded up one of the handles so it touched the knob on top and stood up. He looked around and picked up something from the edge of the herb patch.

"That's a stone," Skylar said.

Gripping the stone tightly, Killin worked that hand into his pocket. Then, he spun around, and with one quick fling, threw the stone, now glowing fiery red, toward the back fence. I heard a yowling screech. Killin turned back to the contraption in the ground, peered at the knob on top, and pulled it out of the dirt. The scene jerked sideways, and I saw plum leaves swish past, followed by a wild cascade of greenery, concrete paths, and red hibiscus flowers as Skylar ran away from Killin Bardis.

"What just happened?" I asked her. "What was that awful noise?"

"Watch again," she said, running the video back a minute. "Look behind him at the fence." She used her fingers to zoom into that part of the image.

This time, I could see that Saffron, our orange cat, was sitting by the fence. When Killin threw the glowing red stone, it splattered into the cat, throwing red sparks in every direction. The yowling had been the last noise Saffron would ever make.

"Aw, no," I said, looking away. "He did not do that."

Skylar didn't bother to answer. It was too sickening. I was about to make a comment about the type of person who would kill an innocent cat when we heard someone tapping at the door. The person tried to turn the doorknob.

I motioned for Skylar to dial 911. "Who is it?" I called out.

"It's Evie. The new daphne plants aren't priced. How much should they be?"

"I'll be there in a minute" (after my heart rate returns to normal). On second thought, I squeezed past Skylar and opened the door. "Evie, did you see a man dressed in black with a ruby stud in his ear?"

"The dish? He just left without buying anything."

Good, he was gone. I looked at Skylar. "Now you can say 'I told you so.'"

"Oh, Hayley. I'm sorry." She put her arms around me.

Chapter 13

"That's the craziest plan I've ever heard," Skylar said. She leaned more of her weight on the pestle she was crushing into a mortar full of basil. She claimed that pulverizing the basil by hand made better pesto sauce than a food processor.

"Do you have a better idea?" I asked her, peering into the toaster oven to make sure the pine nuts weren't about to burn.

"I feel like a better idea exists. I just haven't had that idea yet. Let's go over what we know again."

"Okay, but this is the last time we're going back over what we know. I'll write it down this time." I pulled the tray of pine nuts out of the toaster oven and dumped them into a bowl. Sitting at the kitchen table, I wrote on a yellow pad:

- Lucan Gunter killed by melted stone Buddha and stake through heart.
- Killin Bardis killed Saffron cat with melted stone.
- Melted stones both shriek.
- Killin confronted Lucan before murder.
- Killin said control people by force to keep them from herbs.
- Police won't accept video of killing cat with melted stone as real.

I looked over the list. "I'm not sure it means a lot that both melted stones shriek so bad I can't get anything else out of them. I need to find some white willow bark so I can calm them down. Where am I going to find willow trees in dry Southern California?"

"More importantly, where are we going to find more evidence that Killin Bardis killed Lucan Gunter — evidence the police will accept? They didn't even think the melted Buddha was evidence. And what I mean to say here is, how can we do this without doing something crazy?"

"Here's a not-crazy alternative: If we're absolutely certain that Killin is the perp, we could simply tell Detective Nakamura that we saw him do it."

"Whoa. Take him out with a bald-face lie." Skylar poured the pine nuts into the mortar and ground on them half-heartedly. "That makes me a little queasy. What if we're taking out the wrong guy? That would be terrible. What a horrible idea. How did you even think of that?"

"It's the kind of plan my father would suggest," I said. "You wanted something not-crazy, so there you are."

Skylar stopped grinding altogether and looked at me. "So our possible plans are horrible or crazy."

"I don't think my plan is any crazier than becoming invisible and sneaking into the police station."

"You want to seduce the murderer and get him to confess. That doesn't seem crazier to you?"

"Well, I'm not going to *seduce* him seduce him. I just want to act friendly and see if he'll open up."

"He might not be the one opening up! Remember those ravishing nightmares we had? Don't you think that was Killin Bardis? He invaded our dreams. If he can do that, what else can he do?"

"And what else can we do?" I stood up and paced to the far end of the kitchen, which wasn't far enough. I paced around the other side of the kitchen table. I was literally going in circles.

"We have to do something," I said with my hands in the air. "Otherwise, he comes to visit the herb garden, and we're sitting there waving to him in a friendly way as he goes by. 'Oh hi, Killin. Good to see you again. Who're you going to kill today with a flaming rock?' We're open to him whether we like it or not. I suppose we could close up shop, move away, hope he doesn't come after us. Do you want to try that?"

"No."

"And? But?"

"Hayley, if anything happens to you, I will move to Angels Camp and never be happy again."

"So," I said, staring into the pot of water that was about to come to a boil on the stove. "No pressure."

"All the pressure is from Killin Bardis. Please promise me you won't do anything rash when you're with him."

What was rash when it came to Killin Bardis? If only I knew. I couldn't tell Skylar that the ravishing dream hadn't been a nightmare for me — not until after we discovered that someone had actually been in the house. The idea that the man in that dream had been Killin caused my insides to ache, which made me absolutely furious with myself.

"Bastard!" I hissed.

Skylar jumped.

"Sorry," I said. I looked back at the pot. "The water is boiling."

Skylar dumped pasta into the boiling water. "What makes you think Killin will even engage with you? He hasn't shown that much interest, outside of the nightmare. Face to face, he's been almost hostile."

"Ah, that's where I have an ace in the hole." I pulled the little cloth bag out of my pocket and clattered the stone disk onto the kitchen table. "I think he'll be very interested in that. It might even be the reason he killed Lucan."

"Good. Great." She stopped stirring the pasta. "So he'll kill you for it."

Hadn't thought of that. I backed up to the counter next to the stove and pulled at my T-shirt, looking at the floor. I turned and stared at the little pasta shells swirling in the boiling water.

"How about this," Skylar said. She gave the pasta a quick stir. "Just tell him you know how to get your hands on the stone disk and see what he says. If he gets pushy about it, tell him Detective Nakamura has it."

"Throw Detective Nakamura under the bus."

"He's a cop. He knows how to climb out from under a bus."

"Why would Killin believe I can get my hands on the stone disk if Detective Nakamura has it?"

Now it was Skylar's turn to watch the pasta swirling in the pot. Finally, she said, "How about this: We take a picture of you holding the stone disk. You don't have to explain how you can get it. Be mysterious. Men are attracted to that."

"Says the expert on men. Even I think this plan is getting crazy."

Skylar lifted the pot off the stove and dumped its contents into a colander in the sink. Steam billowed around her head.

"Sometimes," she said, "we have to see crazy as an advantage. That may be our only hope in this case. Also, Mother is working on a spell that might stop Killin if he gets pushy. For that matter, we need a way to stop him so the police can arrest him. Otherwise, he'll kill them with flaming rocks."

# # #

We didn't have to wait long to carry out the crazy plan. While I was at the front desk of the nursery the next morning, Killin came swaggering past. When I glanced up, he looked back at me with the slightest of nods. He didn't smile. I'd never seen him smile.

After he passed and headed toward the herb garden, I whipped out my phone and told Skylar it was time to roll. I locked the cash register and walked as steadily as I could toward the herbs. Skylar was taking a roundabout route, so I didn't want to get there before she was in position to record what happened.

Killin was waiting outside the plywood barrier I'd put up around the herbs. He gestured toward the barrier. "You're fast."

"It's only temporary," I said, spinning the dial on the combination lock. "We don't even have proper hinges on the plywood." I popped open the lock and began to drag one of the big plywood sheets to make an opening.

"Please," he said, stepping up to deal with the plywood. As he was dragging it, I realized that I should have delayed opening the lock. If we went through into the herb garden, Skylar couldn't see us from her hiding place behind the plum trees.

"Killin," I said. He froze as if I'd pulled a gun on him.

"You know my name." As he turned to look at me, light flashed off the ruby stud in his ear.

"Ah, yes, it was on your credit card." I didn't add that I'd seen him on the TV news when the police wanted to question him. That fact didn't seem like a good conversation starter.

"You have me at a disadvantage."

It took me a second to realize what he meant. "Sorry, I'm Hayley. I own the nursery."

"Killin Bardis," he said with the slightest emphasis on the last name. We don't have much use for last names in California. That and his hint of an Irish accent told me he wasn't a native. "Pleasure to meet the famous Hayley West." He inclined his head in the slightest of bows, which made light glint again in the ruby.

"Since you're into herbs," I said, "I wondered if you might be interested in this." I pulled up a photo on my phone of me holding the stone disk. He stopped dragging the sheet of plywood and peered at the photo. If saying his name had caused him to freeze, showing him the stone disk had the opposite effect.

With a sharp intake of breath, he grabbed the phone out of my hand. "Etshigal!" He zoomed in and stared intently at the image of the stone. Then, he looked just as intently at me. "This was in the employ of Lucan Gunter."

"And this phone," I told him, taking back my phone, "is in my employ."

Killin caught my wrist. "You were in league with him."

"Lucan Gunter? No way." I pulled my wrist free and took a step back.

Realization dawned on his face. "Then, this photo was taken after Lucan was killed, and you took Etshigal."

"I didn't *take* Etshigal," I protested. "What's Etshigal? This?" I held up the phone.

"If you don't know what it is, what makes you think it has something to do with the herbs?"

I opened my mouth and closed it again. Did I want to be caught on Skylar's video explaining that I "talked" to stones? And that I'd spent an hour lost in the plant information stored in Lucan Gunter's stone disk? "It's obvious that this stone is intrinsically key to the whole herbal thing," I said, waving my phone. "What's important is that we're clear about what we're about, based on common interests."

"Let's be clear then." He crossed his arms. "Tell me what common interest you suppose we have. What purpose do you have in showing me that photo?"

"Do you want it?"

"Etshigal? Of course I want it."

"What would you give for it?"

He put one hand on his hip and regarded me skeptically. "You're saying you have it?"

"Let's say I can get my hands on it."

Killin passed his hand across his brow. With a sudden fury, he spun around and punched the sheet of plywood behind him. Or at least, I thought he'd punched the plywood. It took me a second to realize that I'd heard no sound. Somehow he'd stopped his fist before it smashed into the wood.

Now he was in my face. "What if someone gets his hands on you, Miss Hayley West? What if someone skewers you like the owner of that stone amulet you think fit for barter? Do you know the rules of this game you're playing? Do you know if there are any rules?"

One of my personal rules is: No spit-shouting in Hayley's face. I stomped on his foot. He grunted and hopped away on his other foot, groaning and cursing. What on earth made me think that dealing with this man would be anything resembling a seduction?

When he'd taken all the names of the holy family in vain, followed by Saint Patrick and Saint Brigid, he paused to breathe, and I told him, "Sorry. You were a little too close."

He hadn't killed me with a molten rock. That was good. I was still alive. Otherwise, my plan wasn't working spectacularly well. If I was going to get him to talk, I'd have to provoke him with something more socially engaging than stomping on his foot — even if I ended up looking like a lunatic in Skylar's video.

He plopped down on the little platform where the stone Buddha used to sit and eyed me as I took a couple of steps toward him. For that matter, I was eyeing him warily, because I thought I might have seen him pick up a pebble.

"Seriously," I told him, "I'm sorry about your foot. I should not have done that."

Still grimacing, he said, "I suppose it's my own fault for getting stroppy in the front row."

"Look, I think I may be able to help you if I understand what you want. I know you can melt rocks. I know you're magic."

He stopped rubbing his foot and cocked his head. "Oh, now, why would you be having a daft idea such as that?"

This was going to look good on Skylar's video: "Because I'm a witch."

"No you're not."

"Yes, I am," I insisted.

"Then do some magic for me."

"Don't be ridiculous. Besides, you wouldn't see anything."

"Why? What's your power? Blinding people with your brilliance?"

I stamped my foot. "If you must know, I can talk to rocks." Oh dear. Why, why, why had I given that away?

For a couple of seconds, the taunting expression lingered on his face. Then his mouth opened. His face went pale. "You're the one they said would come. You twined with Etshigal. That's how you know what's gathered there."

"You know Lucan was looking for herbs? The plants..."

He stood up, wide-eyed. "Yes, yes, you understand. So you know what a terrible beast he was." Killin glanced at the sky and back at me. "You can't imagine how long I followed that man, hoping for an opening to kill him. And then —"

"Police!" The shout came from our right, a dozen feet away.

Killin tucked his right hand into his pocket.

"Keep your hands where I can see them!"

Killin pulled his hand out holding the pebble he'd picked up, now red hot. He turned, swinging his arm.

Skylar shouted, "Stupefy!"

It was not a joke. It had real magic behind it. Skylar had anchored a spell to that word.

Killin's arm slowed. As the hand holding the molten pebble moved like a sloth's, his face shifted from determination to alarm. He slid to a stop with his eyes wide and his mouth frozen in a gaping O.

He couldn't release the red-hot rock.

I stumbled toward him, throwing my arms wide for balance, hoping the officer wouldn't open fire, hoping really hard. On my second stumble-step, I swung sideways and kicked Killin's hand. The molten pebble splattered out of his paralyzed fingers, and the fragments hissed across the concrete walkway.

Spinning to a stop, I faced the officer. His gun was drawn, pointed at my chest. I held my hands away from my body and stood frozen in time, heart thudding, my breath caught somewhere in the past moment when I made a decision that could have cost me my life.

Nobody got shot. Killin had fallen to the ground, but his hand wasn't badly burned. Skylar's Stupefy spell wore off in less than a minute.

The officer cuffed Killin, and while we waited for Detective Nakamura, Skylar told me she'd called 911 when Killin snarled in my face. "I knew you weren't going to put up with that," she told me. "And I was afraid what would happen next."

After hearing from the officer that Killin had admitted trying to kill Lucan Gunter, Detective Nakamura arrested Killin for the murder.

Skylar and I looked at each other in open-mouthed amazement.

She grabbed my shoulders and gave me a little shake. "We did it!" she shouted. "We nabbed the perp!"

Chapter 14

The river of the angels has its source in the confluence of Bell Creek and Arroyo Calabasas, joined by the Browns Canyon Wash flowing south from the Santa Susana Mountains. The river winds lazily along a 51-mile course that's mostly a giant concrete trough.

I had only seen the Los Angeles River in movies, where it usually starred as a location for mayhem. If you were an intergalactic robot or a guy with a muscle car, you somehow felt compelled to find your way into the concrete trough to duke it out. I hoped the trough wasn't as dangerous as it looked in the movies, because I was going into it.

Driving north on the 710 freeway, I couldn't see the river off to my right. It was shrouded in darkness at 4:30 in the morning. I hadn't been able to sleep after my Killin Bardis encounter. Everything about it troubled me. I'd trapped the killer? I should feel good about that. But I didn't.

Killin confessed that he'd been *trying* to kill Lucan Gunter — looking for an opportunity to kill him. If he *had* killed Lucan, why didn't he take the stone disk, Etshigal? Killin wanted it and knew that Lucan had it. Did I interrupt him before he could take it? Detective Nakamura said that Lucan's car keys and wallet were missing, so the killer had time to take those. But the killer did not take Etshigal. It was still hanging from Lucan's neck.

The night after he was arrested, I lay in bed, playing the conversation over and over in my head, tossing and turning, wondering if I was sending the wrong man to death row. Every time I ran through the conversation I could hear my father's voice saying, as he had so many times throughout my childhood, "Life is unfair and unreasonable. Get on with it." But what if it was unfair because I had been unreasonable?

Killin saw Lucan Gunter as a terrible beast that had to be destroyed and thought I was on board with that plan. What if Killin had good reasons to take out Lucan Gunter? Come to think of it, what if Killin was part of some magic police force? There was so much I didn't know.

Most troubling of all was Killin's astonished realization that I was "the one they said would come." I shook my head, trying to shake loose that nutty idea. I stared out the right-hand window into the darkness toward the river and then peered at the map on my phone. I was about to cross over the river, but I still couldn't see it. There was so much I couldn't see.

I turned on the radio. I was willing to be the one who sang along with "The Long and Winding Road" or the one who met the man of her dreams, but being "the one they said would come" did not sound appealing. I was not into the whole destiny thing.

At the moment, I just wanted to find willow trees. They grow along the banks of rivers, which we don't have many of in L.A. The only one that flows year-round was the one I was driving next to. It seemed unlikely that trees could grow in a concrete trough, but I'd heard that up near Glendale the river had a natural bottom.

When I got to Glendale, the sun still wasn't peeking over the San Gabriel Mountains. I had a veggie breakfast burrito at the Narrow Bear Café and joined the early morning joggers straggling along the river's concrete embankments.

There in the bottom of the trough, the river cascaded over rocks, around green islands of shrubs, and past majestic stands of trees. It was a natural landscape, except it was stretched out in a concrete basin. I looked upstream and down. There was not an intergalactic robot or muscle car in sight.

I walked down the steep concrete slope and into a stand of willow trees, and then backed out when I saw that a man was just waking up in there. On my way downstream toward another couple of willows, I picked up a rounded stone from the edge of the river and cradled it in my hands. The impressions from this ancient stone rippled slowly through me — a coyote coming down to the river to drink, giant sloths browsing on sage, people spearing fish with flint points, the smashing water of floods, the dry heat of droughts. In the stone's long telling from deep time, the mountains rose up, rocks wore away.

Voices broke me out of my contact with the stone, and I looked around. A twentysomething man and woman were strolling past me, the woman saying, "My Aunt Bertie can come to the wedding after all. You'll like her. She's traveled to all the places we want to visit and won't talk about them unless you insist." The man laughed. The woman called out, "Amos, don't take Pike in the water."

Behind me, a fat golden retriever splashed along in the shallows. Spread-eagled across the dog's back was a Scottish fold cat, who didn't seem concerned about where the dog went. The couple wandered on upstream, holding hands, making romantic plans, oblivious of me standing there holding a rock in my hand.

The rock's face was smooth and cold. I ran my thumb across it, tracing a vein of quartz. A mammoth had once stepped on this rock with a pack of dire wolves in hot pursuit. I knelt to lay the rock back in the shallows and looked up and down the river. The rock would remember me, just as it did the mammoths and dire wolves. They had all run off into extinction. I stood up and kicked at the water. Easy come, easy go. Get on with it. I continued on downstream toward the second stand of willows.

Looking at what I knew realistically, Killin had been trying to murder Lucan Gunter. That was a fact. He'd said it himself. He was a killer in name and intent. If he got caught for it, that was not my fault.

Except that it *was* my fault — looking at what I knew realistically.

When I reached the trees, I broke off a small branch and stripped away a little of the bark with my fingernails. Sniffing the scraped branch, I got a scent faintly like wintergreen. I licked the wood and twisted my tongue against the nasty bitter bite, like a mouth full of aspirin tablets with a drop of lemon juice added for fun. This was indeed a willow tree.

I began stripping green twigs off the ends of branches. A couple of pre-teen boys came by and were delighted to help me rip twigs off the tree. In a few minutes we had a couple of plastic tote bags jammed full of willow twigs. That would be enough to soothe the melted Buddha at the nursery so I could find out what the stone knew about the murder.

Before that, I was going to do another magic trick: cross L.A. at rush hour. I wanted to see Yorba Linda.

Sitting in traffic on the 5 freeway, I switched from the oldies station to National Public Radio and heard about Killin's arrest for "the so-called vampire murder." We'd made the national news, only this time Killin was getting top billing. The news would bring crowds back to the nursery and café, so I needed to find out what I could in Yorba Linda and get back to work.

The neighborhood where Deedee Piper lived — had lived — was orange groves only a few years ago. A few old ranch-style houses were left from that era. Otherwise, this area now looked like suburbia, with numerous McMansions among the more modest upscale homes (those that had only three-car garages).

Yellow police tape decorated the herbalist's old ranch-style house. As I sat in my car looking at the house, a grade-school boy came trudging along the sidewalk wearing a huge backpack, obviously on his way to school, obviously late. He stopped at the driveway, looked up and down the street, and trotted toward the backyard of the house surprisingly quickly, given the size of his backpack.

I got out and waited for him to come around the far side of the house. When he saw me, he hesitated. I pretended that something scary was behind him and motioned for him to hurry toward me. He glanced over his shoulder and ran in my direction.

Standing on the sidewalk next to me, he looked back and saw that no one was behind him. "What's going on?" he asked me.

"Did you see anything in the house?"

"Nah. Curtains pulled."

"You knew her?"

"The lady? Yeah, I knew her, like, before."

"Before she was killed," I said. "Obviously."

He rolled his eyes at me. "You must be a cop."

"Actually, I'm a witch."

His jaw dropped a fraction of an inch. "Good one," he said.

"So you were saying you knew Ms. Piper?"

"Uh, Deedee, yeah. Before. When she was friendly."

"She wasn't friendly lately?"

"She went spooky. She used to act friendly and show me plants and all."

"How do you mean 'spooky'?"

"You know, strange."

"For example?"

"Like she would stand in her garden with a hoe, not doing anything. She would wave her hand in a circle in the air. I thought at first she was waving to me, but when I waved back, she stood there looking at me, like she didn't know me. So, I thought maybe she had old timer's disease, but she was weird in other ways. Like I'd hear her shouting in her house, you know, moaning and groaning. That was when that vampire was here. That was scary. My dad told me to stay away from that place."

"Vampire? You had a vampire?"

"That one that got killed. My mother said he was a vampire. Now you're a witch. A vampire, a dead woman, then a witch. This neighborhood is getting creepy."

"Wait a minute. You mean the guy who was killed over in Redondo? That vampire?"

"The one who got a stake through his heart."

"He was here?"

"Yeah, he used to visit Deedee. Was she a witch?"

"Mmm," I told him while I was busy thinking. So these two murders were indeed linked. That was why Detective Nakamura was over here.

"At least Deedee didn't turn into a zombie," the boy told me. "Which is lucky. You know her body was lying in there several days before Mrs. Murray found her. Technically, she could have become a zombie."

"Several days. Do you know what day she was killed?"

"Nah. I forget. But I know the vampire was here that day. My dad told me. Mr. Murray's security camera got a vid of the guy going into Deedee's house that day. So he's probably the killer, except the other guy was here, too."

"Another guy? Who was that?"

"Don't know. Mr. Murray might know. He got that guy on his camera, too."

"The Murrays live across from Deedee?"

"Right."

"Thanks for the info."

"Okay."

We had walked to the school entrance. As I turned to go back toward the Murray house, the boy called out, "Ms. Witch!"

I turned around and so did several of the kids who were nearby. Telling people you're a witch really isn't a great idea, even if it does get little boys to talk.

"Something else?" I said.

"Don't mention I was looking in the window, okay?"

"Sure. Our little secret." Which was now shared with a dozen other kids.

"Oh, and you might talk to Mrs. Niedermeyer. I think her doorbell saw the second guy's truck."

"Niedermeyer doorbell, got it."

First, I wanted to see if the Murrays would show me their security camera footage of the two men who visited Deedee Piper. The Murray home was one of the bigger houses on the street. It was the only one with a five-car garage. A maid answered the door. She didn't speak much English, but she let me know that the Murrays no at home and pointed out the ramshackle house where Mrs. Niedermeyer lived.

The only feature of the Niedermeyer home that looked less than a century old was the doorbell. It was a Nest unit with a video camera at the top and a button at the bottom. I pressed the button.

"You here about the kittens?" a woman's voice asked through the doorbell.

"Mrs. Niedermeyer? I wonder if I could…"

"Go away."

"… ask a couple of questions? Please?"

The doorbell was silent. I pressed the button again. She didn't say anything, but I hoped she was listening.

"Kitten, please," I said quickly.

As I was about to bang on the door with my fist and shout, an woman in her 50s with wild gray hair opened the door. "They're in the spare bedroom," she told me, pointing the way through the living room.

The living room was full of video cameras, lights, big-screen TVs, and other equipment. An Oscar sat on top of several DVDs on the mantelpiece. Framed photos of elephants and cheetahs hung on the walls. In the bedroom, the kittens were in a cardboard box on the floor with their mother, an orange and white tabby.

"Nothing special about these kitties," the woman said. "Except they are adorable."

I picked up one adorable kitten and stroked her furry little head with my finger. Skylar and I needed a replacement for the cat that Killin had killed. I looked at the woman to tell her I'd like to take this one. "You're Gret Niedermeyer," I said. I'd seen her on TV.

"Yes," she said, matter of factly. She squinted at me. "Do I know you?"

"You might have seen my face on the news lately. The 'so-called vampire murder' was at my nursery."

"Redondo Beach, yes. You're not here about kittens."

"Correct, although this little girl is changing my mind." I unhooked the kitten's little claws from my shoulder and held her up to look at her furry orange and white face. When I looked back at Gret Niedermeyer, she was pointing a fearsomely big bolt-action rifle in my direction. This was the third time I'd had a gun pointed at me lately, and it was unnerving. This was not something I was going to get used to. I hoped.

"What are you here for?" she asked me.

"The police arrested the wrong man for the murder at my nursery. The death of Deedee Piper is related, and I need to find out how. I'm hoping you can help."

"Why should I trust you?"

Frowning, I thought about that. "Because I'm holding a kitten?"

She almost smiled. Then she nodded decisively, except that she moved her head up instead of down. She leaned the rifle against the wall. "That's as good a reason to trust someone as I'm likely to get. And you picked out my favorite kitten."

I stood up. "You have an awfully big gun."

"I took it from an elephant poacher in Kenya. Then, I shot him with it. I've got the ammo for it around here somewhere." She took the kitten from me and placed her back in the box with her mother. "This little girl can spend a few minutes saying goodbye. Now, what kind of help are you wanting from me?"

"Someone told me that your doorbell saw the pickup truck of a man who was at Deedee Piper's house when she was killed. I'm wondering if I can see what the doorbell saw."

"Only the police know about that. And Jay Gonzalez." She nodded her head upward, as if she had simultaneously thought about Jay and decided he was the one.

"I cannot reveal my sources," I told her. "But Jay was very helpful."

"That boy will be something someday. I'm not sure exactly what. Would you like a cup of tea?"

She ushered me into a kitchen whose back wall was completely covered with awards that had various logos on them: National Geographic, Nature Conservancy, World Wildlife Fund. Two stacks of framed awards lay on a counter. She ran water into an electric kettle and put two of the framed awards on the table. Then, she took cups out of a cabinet and placed them on the awards. "Back in a tick," she said, gesturing for me to sit at the table.

I picked up my cup and looked at the award underneath. It was from the International Union for Conservation of Nature for promoting the protection of the pangolin, whatever that was. A fancy printer on one end of the kitchen counter whirred and shot out a piece of stiff paper. Gret came back and handed me the photo of a pickup truck parked on the street. I squinted at it.

"That's a high-quality print of a low-quality photo from my doorbell," she told me. "Hard to tell a whole lot about it, other than it's a white pickup with a club cab."

"Looks like a big Ford," I said. "Maybe an F350. Wish I could read the company name on the door."

"The police wished that too." She poured hot water in a teapot and set the pot on the table. "I hope you like red bush tea. It's all I have in the house."

"It's fine, thanks. So you didn't see the truck yourself? Or the man who drove it?"

"No, but I think Peg Murray did, or Bradley. They live directly across from Deedee's house."

"The Murrays weren't home when I checked. Do you know if she noticed the name on the truck?"

"Probably not. I'm pretty sure the police talked to her before they got the photo of the truck from me, and they were trying to puzzle out the name from my photo. I don't think they were able to ID the truck or the man who drove it."

Studying the cup in front of me, I thought about what I knew. And what I didn't. Gret said nothing. When I looked at her again, she was studying me. I got the impression she could sit there for hours, watching me as if I were an endangered animal, waiting to see if I would do anything interesting.

"Something about you," she said, half to herself. She stood up to pour the tea. "You remind me of a woman I met in Cuzco. She told me her people were from Machu Picchu. You know the abandoned stone city of the Inca? We were trying to find jaguar in a rocky area north of Abancay, where it was almost impossible to see tracks, and this woman would press her cheek against a boulder and tell me whether a jaguar was using the trail that passed by there. It was uncanny. She was always right." Gret sat down and picked up her cup. "That was many years ago. I wonder if she's still alive. She seemed ancient even back then."

I didn't say anything. What could I say? We sipped our tea.

After a while, I couldn't just sit there. I started rambling through the murder facts. "This murder business has taken over my life. First, Lucan Gunter was killed at my nursery. Or at least, I thought that was first. Now, I'd say it looks like Lucan killed Deedee Piper before that. Or the man with the white pickup killed Deedee, and Lucan just happened to be at her house. So did the white pickup man kill Deedee *and* Lucan? And is Killin Bardis that man? I've seen what he drives. It's not a white pickup."

"Who is Killin Bardis? I don't keep up with the news very well."

"The police arrested him yesterday at my nursery for the murder of Lucan Gunter. I was trying to get him to confess, and he told me he'd been trying to kill Lucan for a long time. A police officer happened to be there."

"So case closed."

"Yeah, well, I'm not so sure. When I was talking to him, I got the impression he thought I killed Lucan."

"And you're pretty sure you didn't."

"Right," I said. "No motive, actually. Killin thinks I know what an evil beast Lucan was, but I hardly know anything about him."

"I'd believe the evil beast story. Deedee Piper was acting strangely in the weeks before she was killed. She went weird when Lucan Gunter began visiting her and got weirder week after week. I think he was doing something to her. I've seen people who were said to be possessed by demons in Africa and South America. Haiti. I wanted to make a documentary about it, but nobody wants to look at it. Offends everybody. Believe what you will, but Deedee seemed like one of those possessed people." Again Gret gave that odd upward nod.

I grimaced. "So Deedee was screaming and writhing?"

"Ah, no, not that kind of possessed. A quieter kind. I suppose it might be better described as *dis*possessed, as if parts of her were pulled out, no longer connected. When I talked to her, she looked over my head and seemed to focus on things I couldn't see. She would reach up and wipe her hand in the air." Gret moved her open hand in a circle, as if she were wiping clean a dirty window.

A chill ran through me. I'd seen that gesture. I'd seen it just the other day. "I have to get home," I told Gret. I stood up. "I have to get home right now."

She stood as well, and I started for the door.

"Do you actually want that kitten?" she asked me.

"Right, the cat," I said turning around. "Yes, please. I need a new kitty for my nursery."

"Did you say someone killed your previous cat?"

"Killin, yes."

"The man you think did *not* murder Lucan Gunter? Sure about that?"

I took a deep breath and let it out. "Honestly, Gret, I'm not sure about anything anymore."

She lifted the kitten away from her mother and handed her to me. "Take good care of this little girl. Don't let that Killin character anywhere near her."

"He's in jail. The kitty is safe. I wish I could say the same for the rest of us."

Chapter 15

When I got back to the Origins Café and Nursery, it was a mob scene. The news that a man named Killin had been arrested there for the "so-called vampire murder" had brought out everybody who hadn't already visited the scene of the crime.

My employees needed help with the customers, but first I wanted to make sure Jade was okay. I drove past the nursery entrance and around the corner to her condo.

When I pressed the button by the door, the first four notes of the Westminster chime played inside and drifted out through the open window. I thought I heard a movement. A funky smell was wafting out the window.

Half a minute went by while I fidgeted, glancing down at Jade's "Welcome to Paradise" doormat, looking at the bird of paradise blooms in the flower bed. No one came to the door.

"Jade?" I called. "Are you in there?"

I knocked and waited. After another minute, getting worried, I turned the doorknob. The door swung open an inch.

"Jade?"

Pushing the door further open, I stepped into the living room and looked around. After the bright sun outside, the dim light in the living room hid everything except the motes of dust swirling in a narrow shaft of sunlight from the window. Water dripped somewhere. I followed the sound to the kitchen, where a pile of dirty dishes sat in the sink. A trickle of water ran from the spigot and dripped down the stack of plates and bowls. I turned off the water and listened. All was quiet. After a moment I noticed a clock ticking. A dog barked across the street.

Jade was a fastidious housekeeper. She would never let dirty dishes pile up. Had she left in a hurry? The pile in the sink looked like days worth of dishes, so something had been wrong for a while.

Peering around the corner into the bedroom, I feared I'd find Jade's lifeless body. The blinds were closed, and the east side of the building was shaded at this time of day. The scant light filtering in showed a bed made up neatly. A dark-wood dresser held several small plants in pots. All the plants were withered and dying. A dusty smell hung in the air. Otherwise, everything seemed to be in its place.

Jade was gone. That was clear. Going away and leaving a stack of dirty dishes in the sink was even more unlike Jade than stacking up dirty dishes in the first place. And she'd left the front door unlocked. She was a floaty kind of person but always responsible — until lately.

Where had she gone? I could give her a call and find out. Duh. Why hadn't I done that already? I took out my phone and touched her mobile number in my contacts list. After a second, I heard "This is the dawning of the age of Aquarius..." playing in the living room — Jade's ringtone. Her phone was in there. I followed the sound.

The phone sounded like it was over in the dimmest corner of the room. With my eyes adjusting to the dim light, I squinted to see past the bright shaft of sunlight that lay along the carpet. And there she was in the dark corner, or what was left of her.

Jade's body was sitting ramrod straight in a high-backed armchair. She was staring straight ahead, vacantly, unblinking. The hairs stood up on the back of my neck.

"I'm too late!" I said out loud.

Her eyes turned slowly toward me, rotating smoothly, like some mechanism driven by inhuman gears, turning, turning. Her head began to turn, too, as though trying to catch up with her eyes.

Even when her gaze had turned in my direction, her head kept turning, and I was terrified for a moment that her head would spin all the way around. But the turning stopped, and her head slowly rotated back to align with her gaze. The whole performance made my skin crawl. It was the eeriest thing I'd ever seen.

"Jade," I whispered.

"There you are," she said with a Southern drawl. "What took you so long, Sugar?"

She had never called me Sugar before. I'd never heard her call anyone Sugar. She'd never had a Southern drawl. She was from right here in Redondo Beach, for goodness sake. And her voice sounded like the voice of a young girl, unless it was the voice of a young boy. It had something *boy* about it. Was I really talking to Jade? Or something else?

"I got here as soon as I could," I told her. "Jade, what's going on? What's wrong?"

She giggled. "Buster likes to growl and bark." Now the drawl was gone, and she sounded like a little girl.

"Damn it!" she shouted, now like a man. She slapped the little table next to her chair. "I told you. I told you. I told you."

Jade reached up into the air, then, and made a motion as though she were wiping clean a dirty window. After staring into the air for a full minute, she leapt out of her chair, grabbed a poker from a rack next to the fireplace, and took up a golf stance. She rocked back and forth on her heels, swung the poker a little, and looked into the distance, which was actually a painting of a mountain hanging over the fireplace.

"This fairway is shambolic!" she cried, and swung the poker with all her might. Somehow she failed to hit anything in the cluttered living room. She raised one hand to shade her eyes in the gloom and stared off at the painting of the mountain. Carefully placing the poker back in the rack, she turned to me and dusted off her hands.

She put a finger on my chest. "I'll have the green beans with hollandaise," she whispered, confidentially. "My mother taught me that. She was a good woman, my mother, though she suffered from the disease of astonishment for the better part of her life." Jade dropped back into the chair again and went rigid.

"Jade," I said, touching her arm, "we need to get you to a safer place."

"Why, Hayley," said a man behind me. "What a pleasant surprise."

I wheeled around, nearly jumping out of my skin. "Bryce," I gasped. My heart was pounding in my chest. "You startled me."

"Oops," he said, with a menacing edge to his voice. Bryce stood something over six feet tall. He was lean and muscular. When he worked on landscaping projects, he didn't expect his Mexican workers to do all the heavy lifting. I'd always thought him a decent man. Now he seemed full of menace.

He stepped around me and went to where Jade sat, putting his hand on her shoulder possessively. "Jade hasn't been feeling herself lately. She really shouldn't be disturbed."

"Sorry," I said, not really feeling sorry. "I think she needs a doctor. Or some kind of help."

"A doctor," he repeated, as if the idea had never occurred to him. He looked up absently. "What a quaint idea." He reached into the air then and moved his hand around as if he were wiping off a dirty window. "Who will give me twenty-five dollars for it? Do I hear twenty-five?"

He looked from me to Jade and back again. He stepped closer. I backed away, but he closed the gap in an instant, his eyes narrow slits. "Twenty dollars going once!" he snarled in my face.

I had to get out of there.

Before I could do anything, Bryce swung away and spoke again, only this time he sounded like a child, a little boy with a Southern drawl. He'd never had a drawl before. "Ya'll don't fret. Everything will be taken care of."

He let out a man-sized yell, something like "Yee-ha!" Taking both of Jade's hands, he lifted her from the armchair, and they launched into a jerky square dance in the living room.

"Swing your partner!" Jade shouted, as Bryce flung her against the coffee table.

"Promenade!" Bryce yelled, sounding like a little boy again. "Give me twenty-five for it!"

When they high-stepped to the far end of the living room, I dashed out the front door. From the sunlit sidewalk, I could hear them shouting inside, only now they sounded like teenagers singing, "Old Dan Tucker was a mean old man. He washed his face in a frying pan. He combed his beard with a wagon wheel, and he died with a toothache in his heel."

# # #

Glad to escape to the relative sanity of the mob scene at Origins Café and Nursery, I reassured myself that Jade was alive and dancing. I had to find out more about what was going on there. In the meantime, I hurled myself into the task of dealing with customers who were mostly coming out of ghoulish curiosity about "the so-called vampire murder."

Call me crass, but I wished I'd ordered more T-shirts the night before. If you're going to deal with hordes of rubberneckers, you might as well sell them T-shirts. I learned this deep philosophy at my father's knee. He had made boat loads of money by the time I was a teenager, but I never saw him balk at the chance to make another dollar.

Impatient to be doing other tasks, I diverted my attention by counting the number of T-shirts I was not selling. Each time I dealt with a customer I'd never seen before, I tallied another T-shirt sale I couldn't make because I was out of T-shirts. After my tally of unsold T-shirts ran into the dozens, I lost interest in anything other than getting customers out the door. By the end of the day, I'm sure they found me rude. I felt bad about that. My father would never feel bad about being rude. I'm proud to have that difference between us.

When I'd hustled the last gawker out of the nursery, I found Skylar in the café and brought her up to date on what I'd discovered in Yorba Linda and at Jade's.

"So I learned a lot," I concluded. "But I don't understand any of it."

"Your description of Jade and Bryce sounds like *Invasion of the Body Snatchers*, except in this case the snatchers have personalities."

"Multiple personalities, and some of them are from the South. Has Jade ever called you Sugar?"

"Nobody has ever called me Sugar."

I was about to protest that that couldn't possibly be true, when I realized that it probably was. "In any case," I told her, "both Jade and Bryce had the Southern accent at different times, and both of them sounded like little boys."

"Can we guess that some little boys in Atlanta hacked into their brains?"

"That's the only logical explanation. Unless you believe in multiple-personality possession."

"Mother says there's no such thing as possession," Skylar told me.

"Your mother should see Jade and Bryce. I wonder if she'd change her mind about possession. They sure seemed possessed to me."

"Just bear in mind that you're prejudiced in favor of magical explanations."

"What do you mean? I'm struggling to have any explanation at all."

"Right, but here's the problem: Once you know about magic, it's the easy solution for any puzzle. You get lazy and jump to that conclusion. 'Oh, I don't understand what's going on, so it must be magic.'"

"So you're saying I'm lazy?" I bristled at the very idea. I'd been struggling to solve the murder and take care of business since before dawn, and I was lazy? "You're unfair. And that's why nobody calls you Sugar, by the way."

I didn't need to see the hurt look on Skylar's face to know I'd been unfair myself. "I'm sorry. That was mean." I rubbed my eyes. "I'm worn out. And I don't mean for that to sound like an excuse, even though I hope it is."

"You want me to make a rock balm from your willow twigs?" she asked me.

All right, she wasn't going to forgive me right away, and I couldn't blame her. "Yes, please."

She stuffed a bunch of the willow twigs in her industrial-strength food processor and pulverized them down to the molecular level. That made her feel better. The directions for the "rock balm" spell called for marinating the twigs in mineral oil for several weeks. Who had time for that? Skylar added oil as she buzzed the twigs and ended up with a fine wintergreen-scented paste.

When she was done, she scraped the paste into a bowl. "Ready when you are," she told me.

Walking back to where the melted Buddha was, I asked her, "Skylar, if I don't jump to the conclusion that Jade and Bryce are possessed, what other explanation is there?"

"Blow me if I know," she said. "I was just passing on the wisdom that Mother gave me years ago. Maybe Jade and Bryce ate magic 'shrooms."

"Okay, well, that's still a magic explanation."

"Very funny. Let's see if you can get something out of this puddle of rock." She spread the willow paste on the melted Buddha like peanut butter. We finished the spell by reciting a little story forward and backward:

> The sandbar of morning emerged from the ocean of night, washed by waves of mist that arrived from a distant reach. The sound of water lay upon everything. For a moment the mist was still, and then the sun broke through.

Gingerly, I put my fingertips into the willow butter so they were just touching the rough surface of the melted Buddha. I didn't feel the shrieking I'd felt before. I didn't feel anything. I rubbed my hands into the paste to get more contact with the stone. Nothing. Had our soothing spell erased the stone's memory?

"Do you think we could wash off the willow stuff now?" I asked Skylar. "I need to put my bare hands against the stone. Everything feels quiet in there. Too quiet."

"Let's give it a try," she said. She found a hose and washed off my hands and the stone.

Squatting in the patch of mud we'd just made, I put both hands on the lump of stone that had once been a Buddha. Impressions began to come. Slowly, slowly, I felt water flowing by. This must have been in Thailand, since the Buddha had been carved there. A long time ago, the stone was a small boulder by a stream. Something furry sat on the stone. A monkey? Something wet and warm plopped on the stone and ran down the side.

"Aw, crap." I took my hands off the stone and sat back on my heels.

"What?" Skylar looked alarmed.

"A monkey pooped on this stone."

Skylar put her hands on her hips. "Now, Hayley dear, we're going to have to bear down here and not let a little monkey dookey get in the way of progress."

"This was a lot of monkey dookey," I complained. I put my hands back on the stone. The stone was "talking" much slower than stones usually did, which was pretty slow. And it was ignoring my nudges to tell about recent events. After a while, my legs got tired, so we dragged the stone to a dry spot where I could sit. I sat and sat and sat, and finally stood up.

"I'll get old and gray and never get past this rock's first million years in Thailand," I told Skylar. "The willow worked way too well. This rock is completely stoned."

"Seriously?"

"Sorry."

"Maybe the rock will be less zonked tomorrow," Skylar said.

"I'll try again then. In the meantime, we need to talk to your mother about Jade."

Our new kitten wandered over and attacked a bug crawling next to the rock.

"You're a cute little critter," Skylar told the cat.

"Let's put the rest of the willow butter on the rock that Killin used to bash our poor Saffron cat."

"If you'd seen him do it, you'd know he's the murderer. I lost my breakfast after I saw that."

"Seeing your little phone video was bad enough," I assured her.

"You don't want to talk to that rock, do you?"

"Not really. Except it might tell us something about Killin. Do you think?"

"One way to find out."

Skylar scraped the last bit of willow butter out of the bowl and smeared it on the splattered remains of the rock that Killin had melted. We stood 20 yards from the rock to recite the little story forward and backward, hoping the extra distance would keep the rock from totally blissing out. That's the kind of dumb logic that can work with magic spells.

When we finished reciting backwards, I picked up the flattened rock and found it positively chatty compared to the melted Buddha. The impressions jumped around from a rock quarry with rumbling dump trucks to various people walking by in the nursery. This rock was all fun and games.

Then it hit something evil. The rock went haywire with revulsion at about the same time it melted. The impressions were jumping around, so I had trouble teasing out the sequence.

Confused by what the rock was giving me, I put it back on the ground. "It's unclear whether the rock was thrown by someone evil or hit something fiendish or both," I told Skylar.

"Seems clear to me," she said. "Do you suspect that our cat was fiendish? Have we got down to suspecting everybody, including the cat?"

"Just letting you know what the rock says. It was upset about being melted, of course."

"Who wouldn't be?"

"Its fury carries right through until it cools, and the whole episode has a dollop of nastiness on top. Normally, I don't think it would be bent out of shape just because it bashed an animal. Rocks don't really care about living things that way. They don't recognize evil the way we do. But they have a sensitivity to deviations in the natural order that goes right down to the bedrock of reality. So to speak."

"So to speak," Skylar repeated doubtfully.

"This rock is appalled at what happened."

"What did happen? Your description is like one of those movie trailers that leaves me wondering what on earth the movie is about."

"Well, I haven't seen the whole movie either, okay? It's all confused, and I'm comparing what I sense with what I think I should be sensing. If Killin is evil, the rock should be giving off bad vibes when the sequence starts. Instead, I feel that later. I think."

"Which means that our cat Saffron was evil? I've certainly felt that way about cats in general, but Saffron was a very mellow cat."

"Can cats be possessed? Otherwise, it doesn't make sense."

"There you go again with the possession theory."

"At least it's clear we're dealing with magic here."

Skylar agreed almost reluctantly. "To tell you the truth, possession is a topic Mother never wanted to discuss. She got all twitchy when I brought it up. She would say I'd been watching too many bad movies and change the subject."

"So it could happen?"

"I don't know! I suppose the answer *could* be yes, only because the topic made Mother so uncomfortable. But please let me point out that you might be jumping to another conclusion here, and I am not suggesting you are being lazy."

"What are you suggesting?"

"That you're smitten with that man, and you're grasping at any straw that lets him off for smashing our cat with a melted rock."

"Smitten? Smitten?" I spun in a circle waving my hands. "I'm trying to be fair. I'm trying to *not* jump to conclusions. Has that occurred to you?"

When I stopped turning I saw that Skylar had her hands on her hips, smirking at me — smirking at me with an eye-roll on top. She didn't say anything.

I put my hands on my hips and glared back at her.

Then, she dissed me by taking out her phone and ignoring me completely. I waited her out. I started thinking about what a funny word "smitten" is. I started feeling unsettled when I remembered it means to be hit with something.

"This is freaky," Skylar said. She looked up from her phone. I looked back at her. She looked at her phone. "Bryce's Facebook page mentions he's from Macon, Georgia. He moved to L.A. when he was in his thirties."

We stared at each other a while longer.

"What are you saying?" I asked her.

"That Bryce must have grown up with a Southern accent."

"That means Bryce is possessed by his younger self? And so is Jade?"

"Let's don't jump to any conclusions."

We shared a rueful laugh.

"I have no idea what's going on," I told Skylar.

"Me neither, but I'll bet it has something to do with magic. What do we do now?"

"Talking to Killin might be useful. Do you think they'll let me visit him in jail?"

"A murder suspect? And you're involved in the case? I don't think they'll be fond of the idea."

"I'll have to sneak in again."

Chapter 16

Putty-colored walls, functional furnishings, and no iron bars in sight. Jail was nicer than I expected. The main lockup was clean and modern. Certainly it was the nicest jail I'd ever been locked up in, since it was the only jail I'd ever been in for any reason.

I peeked through the windows in the doors of several cells and mostly saw men working on laptop computers. One wore headphones and seemed to be editing music. Did this jail offer free Wi-Fi?

The prisoners' names were posted outside their cells. That should have made it easy to find Killin, but after running up and down the rows of cells on the ground floor, I hadn't seen his name. I trotted invisibly up the stairs to the second level and ran past all the cells. No Killin.

It made sense that they'd keep a murder suspect separate from the men serving time for a DUI or malicious littering, but where? Back on the ground floor I waited outside a corridor with a locked door until I could pass through with a guard. When that door slammed behind me, I now had three locked doors between me and the outside.

At least, that's what I thought until I realized I'd taken another route out of the lockup. The jail was more complicated than I thought. Then a whiff of coffee brewing gave me an idea. The jail's kitchen was easy enough to find. If they had Killin locked in a separate area, somebody would take breakfast to him.

One kitchen worker had a list with Killin's name on it, so I stuck to that guy like glue. Eventually, he plopped a carton of milk, a box of cereal, and a cup of coffee on a tray and left it at a small guard station around the corner.

The guard there touched the screen on his desk and waited. A few minutes later, two more guards came. Each of them waved their badges in front of a gray box by the steel-and-glass door and carried the tray through, with me hot on their heels. The door slammed shut behind me. We were now in a small area facing another steel-and-glass door. The guards waved their badges again, and the lock on this door clicked. Once we were all through, the door slammed behind me. I wiped my invisible clammy hands on my invisible pants. Once I got in, how would I get out?

This corridor had four cells on it, three of them empty. One guard peered through the little window in the door of Killin's cell. That guard waved his badge in front of the gray box, and the door lock clicked a couple of seconds later. The guard with the tray opened the door and went in, but the other guard stood back from the door. He was a big guy, and he took up most of the available space. I squeezed between him and the opposite wall. Then I shoved the other guard as he was coming out of the doorway so I could scoot around him.

The second guard swayed, scratched his side, and looked at his watch. It's amazing what you can get away with when you're invisible. People really aren't paying much attention to what's going on around them, even when they're supposed to be on guard.

The guard slammed the door shut behind him. That was the final door for me. I was well and truly locked in.

The breakfast tray was resting at the end of the single bunk in the narrow cell. Sitting at the other end of the bed was Killin Bardis.

He was staring doubtfully at the tray. "How about a bowl?" he shouted toward the closed door.

"The little cereal box tears open so you can use it as a bowl," I told him.

He didn't even jump. He picked up the cereal box and examined it. "Snap, crackle, pop," he read. "Is this food?"

"Carbs," I told him. "But not pure sugar. They could have given you something even sweeter."

"They could have given me the full Irish. I'm not eating this rubbish." He dropped the box of cereal back on the tray and picked up the coffee.

"How did you know I was here?"

"I saw when you shoved past the guard. I expected you yesterday. What took you so long?"

So the guard I shoved past hadn't noticed, but Killin did. Who was I dealing with here? "You knew I had an invisibility spell and would use it to come talk to you?"

"Any decent witch has an invisibility spell, and it was easy to tell you didn't know what was going on. You seemed the type who'd come looking for answers. Is it true you ken the stones?"

"Ken? As in understand?"

He nodded.

"Yes, I'm the *type* who talks to stones. Is it true you killed Lucan Gunter?"

He put the coffee cup down, got off the bed, and paced two steps, which was the entire length of the cell. I squeezed against the wall to stay out of his way. "It's true I wanted to kill Lucan Gunter. It's true I was going to kill him. The only reason I didn't was because I didn't have a good opportunity, and it would have been inconvenient to have it blamed on me. Now someone's robbed me of the pleasure of killing him, and yet it's blamed on me anyway. Thanks to you, as it turns out."

"Sorry. We thought you were the murderer, and we didn't think the police would figure that out on their own."

His brow furrowed. "You mean you purposely trapped me into saying I wanted to kill Lucan?"

"We thought you were the murderer! We were afraid!"

"So that damp-knickers look you were giving me was really your 'I see a murderer and I will get you' look? Is that a turn-on for you? Trapping men with your come-hither look?"

"I do not have a come-hither look. *You* have a come-hither look."

"And that frightened you, I suppose."

"What frightened me was knowing that a stone Buddha was melted in Lucan Gunter's death, and then you melted a rock to kill my cat."

He stopped pacing directly in front of me and looked in my direction. "A stone Buddha was melted?"

"I thought you were the type who knew what was going on."

He was also the type who would simply ignore a jab like that.

"And by the way," he said, "I did not kill your cat."

"My friend Skylar has you on video killing our cat, so there's no point denying it."

"Ah, you see, we've got to an area where you don't know what's going on. I killed an agent of Fel Dinaden who was disguised as a cat. Specifically, your cat. Apparently."

"So my cat was possessed by this Fel Dinaden person? Who was evil?"

"Evil all around, yes, but not possessed. That's impossible. And not possessed by Fel, but by an agent of Fel. I mean *not* possessed by an agent of Fel."

"Was it Fel or his agent who killed Lucan Gunter?"

"*Her* agent, and no, they didn't kill him. I don't know who killed Lucan. I wouldn't really care so much who did it if everyone would give up the idea that it was me."

"I don't think they're going to give up that idea unless *someone* can find out who really did do it. Too bad this is an area where you don't know what's going on."

He rubbed his chin. "Let's say I walk back my smarter-than-thou comment. Would you be willing to help me?"

"That's why I'm here, Killin."

He took a self-satisfied sip of coffee. "So my come-hither look was not completely wasted."

After rolling my eyes, I looked around for a clock. Finding the right cell had taken a while. I needed to be thinking about how to get through all the locked doors between me and the outside world.

"What time is it?" I asked him. "I need to go before my invisibility spell wears off."

"Relax. You just got here. You're good for all day, aren't you?"

"No, less than three hours."

"What kind of newt did you use?" he asked incredulously.

"No newt at all. I'm a vegan witch."

He got halfway through an eye roll before his mouth formed a long "Ohhhh" and he looked off into a corner of the cell. "That's why you have all those unusual herbs, and that's why Fel wants to know what you're doing."

"Who is this Fel person?"

"That's a long story. Better not get into that if time is short. Let's talk about getting me out of here."

"What would you suggest I do to find the perp?"

"To tell you the truth, I don't know where to look for the perp. What you say about the melted Buddha means the killer must be magic."

"That's what we figured."

"I'll be blasted if I know another witch or sorcerer who's willing to take on an agent of Fel's. Having someone do that would be wonderful news on the one hand and horrifying on the other. We don't need another faction butting in with violence."

"Are you saying that Lucan Gunter was an agent of Fel?"

"Right."

"And this Fel is a bad, evil person?"

"Powerfully bad."

"So whoever killed Lucan would also have to be powerful? And this person might be using his or her power for good or might be vying for power over Fel? Either way, I have no business mixing it up with a person like this."

"Correct," Killin said. "Like the way you challenged me the other day? Don't do that. Just see if you can find out anything else about what happened and be wary. Drat!" He pounded his fist on the little table. "I need to get out of here to deal with this. In the meantime, do you have any other clues you haven't told me about?"

"I was going to ask you about some odd behavior, but I've got to get out of here."

"Tell me quick."

"My friend Jade has gone weird. Her personality jumps around like she's doing impressions of different people. Same for her boyfriend. I was given the same description of an herbalist who was killed in Yorba Linda, Deedee Piper. Each of them did this odd behavior where they'd reach up and move their hand around as if they're wiping off a dirty window."

"Ravishing," Killin said. "I know Lucan was ravishing Deedee Piper, probably Jade too. She's the herbalist in Redondo Beach?"

"Right. So, that's it — the ravishing."

"You know about that?"

Nodding uncertainly, I held up two fingers a quarter inch apart to show that I knew a little. Killin couldn't see the invisible girl doing any of that, so I said, "I've heard of it." I didn't mention that I'd been ravished myself.

"Have you heard that ravishing can include sex?" Killin asked. "They say it's the best sex you can have, by the way. Lucan was using it to find out what these herbalists knew, because it allowed him to look directly into their souls. Unfortunately, that can knock loose parts of the person's psyche, causing the parts to reconnect in random ways."

"Lucan was doing this? But Lucan's dead. Jade has gotten worse since he was killed."

"So someone else is doing it." He stood up and started taking the items off the plastic food tray. "You have to find that person."

He took the tray to the door of his cell and pounded it against the glass window, shouting, "Help!"

He paused to say to me, "Lucan had a ring that gave him the power to ravish. Whoever killed him might have taken the ring." He looked out the window into the corridor and contorted his face, shouting again. We waited. All was quiet.

"Killin, no one is coming. How am I going to get out?"

"Oh, they're coming. They've got video cameras all over the place, so they know I'm calling for help. I could be choking to death in here, and they'll take their sweet time coming to help."

Sure enough, the hallway door slammed, and two guards appeared outside his cell. He stood back from the door and doubled over. When one guard opened the door, Killin gasped that he felt like his insides were splitting open.

"Can you walk?" the guard asked, taking a pair of handcuffs off his belt.

"I think so," Killin said. He turned sideways so the guard could put on the cuffs. As I edged out the door of the cell, I heard him call out, "The ring has a blue crystal in it. Look for the ring."

"Delirious," muttered the guard in the hallway. He said into the microphone on his lapel that they were bringing Killin to the infirmary.

I went out through the doors at the end of the corridor with the guards and Killin. My pants were starting to become visible, my famous plaid pants. I hadn't been able to find anything else that worked as well. Now the pattern of the fabric was shimmering in the air like a plaid ghost. But as usual, nobody in the building noticed as I trotted through the corridors. I might be okay so long as I didn't run into any eagle-eyed Girl Scouts.

Tucking in tight behind a couple of officers who were chatting their way out the front door, I got out of the building and ran for a clump of trees at the corner of a nearby apartment complex. None of the people on the sidewalk thought it peculiar that an empty outfit was running past them, though a couple of dogs gave me puzzled looks. Skylar wasn't parked where I'd left her. I rooted around in a clump of bottlebrush until I found the phone I'd hidden there, and she came for me in a few seconds.

On our way back to the nursery I told her that I now knew how to find the perp. "All we have to do is look at every finger in L.A. until we find one with a blue crystal ring on it."

"You have a wonderful way of simplifying a complex task," she told me, admiration resounding in her voice. "With a population of four million, that's only 40 million fingers to look at — fewer than that if you figure that some people don't have the full 10. Let's start now, shall we?" She held up her fingers.

"No blue crystal," I said. "Only 39 million and something to go." I held up my own fingers but couldn't see them.

Chapter 17

Somewhere, a finger was wearing a blue crystal ring. Where was that finger? The place to start looking for clues was obvious. If only we didn't have day jobs, we could check immediately.

In truth, I loved my day job. Working at the nursery was wonderful so long as nobody was murdering anybody or parading through to have a look at where a murder had taken place. In other words, my day job had been great until somebody bashed Lucan Gunter in the head and drove a stake through his heart.

"We're sure Killin isn't the perp, are we?" Skylar said as she locked up the café for the day.

"I'm buying his story that the cat he killed wasn't really our cat. It was some kind of evil agent."

"Sure looked like our cat."

"And I look like thin air when we run the invisibility spell. What kind of magic does it take to disguise yourself as a cat?"

"I know it can be done, but I don't know how," Skylar admitted, as she got in my car. "I'd guess it takes a lot of go juice because you're transforming a big body to a creature ten times smaller."

Starting the engine, I asked, "By 'go juice' you mean lots of newts and frog toes?"

"Right, or lots of personal power, the kind that takes years off your life. You remember how long it took me to recover when I made the plants grow so I could rescue that guy on the mountain?" Skylar had spent several days in bed after that exploit.

I nodded and backed the car out of its parking space. "I was wondering about magical energy the other day, actually. When I talk to a stone, I sometimes end up a little tired, but that's mostly because it takes so long and fills me up with so many impressions. Why doesn't it sap my energy? Why don't I spend days recovering like you did?"

"It's the difference between listening and directing. It takes hardly any energy for me to listen to plants, the same as when you listen to rocks. Directing plants to grow quickly, like I did on the mountainside, is a different deal. Takes way more energy. I'm surprised Mother didn't talk to you about that because you might be able to direct rocks the way I can direct plants."

"Direct rocks to do what?"

"I don't know. It's your magic. You have to puzzle it out."

"But it doesn't make sense to direct rocks. They just lie there."

"It's magic! Play with the idea next time you talk to a rock. But before you do that, talk to Mother about energy. If you use too much of it, you get to the point where you can't pay it back."

About to drive out of our parking lot, I put my foot on the brake. "It's like a bank account?"

"Or maybe like a battery. I don't know. That's why you need to talk to Mother. In the meantime, don't get carried away with the energy thing."

"Safety tip. Got it," I told her. "So turning yourself into a cat would risk overdrawing your account?"

"Yep. It's a complicated, high-power spell that's dangerous — besides the risk that somebody will bonk you with a flaming rock. You've got no guarantee that the spell will simply wear off. Changing back to your own body might take a lot more energy and require a human being to run the undo spell for you."

"It's scary to think that somebody would take that risk just to spy on us," I reflected.

"Good point. For our own peace of mind, it would be better if we refuse to buy the evil agent story. Otherwise, we have to believe that a super-power bad guy wants something from us."

"Remember our sex dreams? Your mother was right. That had to be the ravishing Killin told me about."

"Does he know so much because it was him doing it?"

Deep down in my belly, part of me wanted Killin to be the one; it really did. But what I said was, "Why would he do it to Jade and Bryce?"

"Why would anybody do it to anybody?" she retorted. "We don't know anybody's motivation here. We know that Killin wanted to kill Lucan Gunter. But do we know why?"

"Because Lucan was evil. That's what Killin told me."

"I know lots of evil people, but I don't go around killing them. What kind of person is Killin Bardis that he takes it upon himself to kill somebody?"

"You ask hard questions, and I'm famished. After we get some dinner, let's go see if Jade can tell us who's wearing the ring with the blue crystal."

#

We were surprised when Jade answered the door, and for a few seconds I thought she was back to normal. She seemed all perky and glad to see us. Then, I realized she was perky and glad like a completely different person.

"Land sakes," she was saying. "Ya'll come on in. Let me stir us up some lemonade. It's hotter than a blister bug in a pepper patch, ain't it?"

It wasn't any kind of hot, but we went in. Her condo was pitch black dark inside, and the light switch didn't do anything. Skylar and I got our phones out for light and found a floor lamp that worked.

By the time we got the light on, Jade was sitting in her easy chair, all thoughts of lemonade forgotten. She went catatonic for a moment. With a brief shudder, she laughed gaily and clapped as though she were at the circus. "Well done!" she shouted. She hesitated, reaching up to wipe at an invisible window. Looking at the floor, she said in a man's voice, "Don't you dare."

Skylar and I looked at each other.

"We're not likely to get anything useful out of her," I said.

"Not even lemonade," Skylar said. "You weren't exaggerating about her condition. We need to get her some help."

"Prozac and talk therapy aren't going to fix this problem, are they? She needs magical help, and where do we get that?"

"We'll have to find out. In the meantime, I think she'll be safer in the psych ward than here alone."

"If she is alone," I said. Skylar called Bryce's name and went to look through the condo.

I crouched in front of Jade's easy chair and looked up into her face. She was squinting, as though trying to make out a distant scene that didn't exist in the room, and she kept smacking her tongue off the roof of her mouth. "Jade," I said softly, "have you seen a man wearing a ring with a blue crystal in it?"

Her face softened and her gaze wandered blankly around the room. She closed her mouth and scratched at her cheek. Then, she fixed on me briefly before her eyes closed and her mouth fell open in a moan. "The men enter me. They want everything."

"Men? More than one? Is one of them wearing a blue crystal ring?"

She was moving her head in a circle with her eyes closed, murmuring words that I gradually realized were the names of cities. "...Idaho Falls, Cincinnati, Coral Gables, Bend..."

Skylar returned to the living room. "Boy, the kitchen is a mess. No sign of Bryce."

I put my hand on Jade's arm. Her eyes snapped open and she snatched her arm away. "What's the idea, mister?" she demanded in a boy's voice.

"Sorry. Jade, do you know where Bryce is?"

"Landscaping yard," the boy said matter-of-factly.

"He's landscaping a yard?"

She guffawed and slapped her knees. "No, silly. He's at his place 'a bidness."

"Do you think you could show us the way there?"

"Shore! Let's get outta this dump." She put her hand on the top of my head and sprang from the chair. She was out the door before Skylar and I knew what was happening. We found her outside in the flower bed gazing at the sky.

"What happened to the stars?" she said in a little girl voice.

"They're up there," Skylar assured her. "Let's go find Bryce."

"But it's all a gray smudge," Jade complained.

"Welcome to L.A.," Skylar said. She guided Jade to the car.

While I drove, Skylar prompted Jade. "Which way to find Bryce?"

"Bilbo Baggins will know," she said and giggled. I was ready to give up and go back to the nursery so we could look up the business name that Bryce operated under. That's when she surprised us by saying, "Left at Melrose, left at Montague, right on Dunbar till you reach Allistar Industrial Park."

We were so unprepared for the detailed directions, we didn't catch the first couple of turns, but we got the name of the industrial park. We looked it up and were there in a few minutes.

It was a big place with several rows of corrugated metal structures on either side of driveways. Most of it was dark. People had gone home for the day. At the end of one driveway, a gate stood open. A white pickup was parked just inside the gate.

I eased closer until my headlights lit up the side of the truck. It was an F350. Lettering on the door of the cab said "El Dorado

Landscaping" with other info beneath that. I remembered now that Bryce operated under that name.

"That's Bryce's truck," I told Skylar.

Digging in my purse, I found the photograph that Gret had printed for me. Though it was impossible to read the name on the pickup truck in the photo, the shape of the lettering was a perfect match for the truck sitting in front of us.

Passing the photograph to Skylar, I said "Gret Niedermeyer's doorbell took this photo. It shows that truck parked near Deedee Piper's house at the time of her murder." I backed up 20 yards, cut my headlights, and turned off the engine.

Skylar pursed her lips. "That means... What does that mean?"

"Lucan Gunter and Bryce were both at Deedee's at the time she was killed. Lucan was seen going into her house. The man driving that truck in front of us was seen going around the back of her house."

"So it's easy to guess that one of them killed her," Skylar observed. "But which one? And later, somebody killed Lucan. Bryce could have killed them both."

"It could have been Bryce," echoed Jade in a child's voice.

"Or it could have been somebody else, somebody wearing a blue crystal ring," I said.

"Did the police figure out it was Bryce's truck that was at Deedee's?"

"I don't think so."

"We could go tell the police and let them deal with it."

"Could be Bryce," Jade sang. "Could go. Police, please."

"Yeah, what she said," Skylar told me. "Let's buzz Detective Nakamura and tell him it was Bryce at Deedee's."

"Police, please," Jade sang. "Bryce at Deedee's."

I put my hand on Skylar's arm. "We already set up Killin to be arrested for Lucan's murder, and I don't think he's guilty. He's sitting in jail instead of helping us find the real killer. Do we really want to blow the whistle on Bryce? He's clearly a victim here, too.

He had symptoms like Jade's. What if he was trying to stop Lucan and never hurt anybody?"

"Come on," Skylar said. "Bryce has always been a jerk."

"He's never been magical," I insisted. "And if Bryce knows who has the blue crystal ring, we need to find that out." I opened the car door and got out. "I'm going to see if he can tell me. You get in the driver's seat and be ready to get out of here. If I'm not back in ten minutes, call the police."

"I'll come with you," Skylar said, opening her door.

"You need to stay with Jade. We don't want her running off in the state she's in."

Bryce's storage yard was pitch dark. Despite the lingering warmth of the June evening, I shivered. Strange shapes loomed all around me. I pulled out my phone and started the flashlight app. The shapes next to me were stacks of plastic pots. I patted them. Good, not giant snakes. A tangle of irrigation hoses lay next to the pots.

Outside the circle of light, the strange shapes marched into obscurity in the outer darkness. And who might be noticing my light? Bryce and only Bryce? I put the phone away.

Now I could see less than ever. I waited, listening. What were Bryce's intentions? I edged past the irrigation tubing, and my leg scraped against something rough — a pile of broken paving stones, from the feel of them. I felt my way around them. Why hadn't I left my car headlights on? Something big loomed on my right. I felt rakes and other tools. They were on the side of a yard-service trailer. On my left was a Bobcat that had a long digger arm attached to it. A street light in the distance glinted off the scoop on the end of the arm. Those diggers made Bobcats look like giant scorpions.

A man's silhouette passed across the gap between the trailer and the Bobcat. What was Bryce doing here in the dark? Was it Bryce? What if somebody else had taken Bryce's truck? Or what if he had several of those trucks for his landscaping business? I could be facing anybody out here. Why hadn't I thought of all this sooner?

Why hadn't I thought of it before I ventured into this dump yard in the dark?

I moved to keep the Bobcat between me and the man I'd glimpsed, straining to hear his movements. Everything was quiet. Then metal scraped against metal a few feet from me, and the Bobcat roared to life. The headlights came on, blindingly bright. I backed away and held my hand in front of my eyes.

"Bryce?" I shouted. "It's me, Hayley. Could you turn off the lights?"

Edging toward the trailer to my right, I tried to get it between me and the light, but as I got next to it, one of the weed whackers hanging on it started up. In a few seconds, another one started. Their cutting lines ripped the air in front of me. Then, one of the blowers in the trailer started, and a cloud of dust billowed around me. Blinking and coughing, I backed up. On the other side of the trailer, the digger on the back of the Bobcat clanked into the air. The scoop hung high overhead, wobbling in place. Now a lawnmower roared to life. A chainsaw. The devil's own yard service was whining and screeching and ripping around me.

I'd lost my bearings, but I turned away from the main part of the racket and ran. I didn't get far. In an instant, the world went from loud and frightening to quiet and eerie. Light rose up around me, shimmering pale green and violet, rent with black bubbles that slowly rose through the air, as thought the air itself had turned into a thick fluid. One of the bubbles burst into yellow ooze with a malignant sighing sound — "kah." More bubbles rose and burst, each going "kah" and staining the air yellow.

I rose slowly. My feet tread the air, thick now like molten amber, like running in a dream in which you can't possibly run, and really my will to run was ebbing away, so why continue to try? This useless running. So much was meaningless, the movement of my feet, the bills that needed paying, the loss of my mother, the feeling of my breath as it rose and fell, the ultimate certainty of my own death.

Lifting my careless arms, I saw that I wore incandescent blue robes that swirled around me in a wind I couldn't feel, as the shadowy bubbles burst listlessly, kah, kah-kah, kah. I began to turn around, very slowly at first. The only meaning was in movement, because I knew that farther along in my turning I would reach the angle of understanding at which my sight would pierce the veil. All would be clear. All would be certain. Soon I would see. The portal would open.

I reached up into the flowing light and wiped away the haze with the palm of my hand so I could see.

The light penetrated me then, pressed me upward, coiled in me like a skein of wind. This was almost complete. My robes of blue light ruffled around me, purling in the luminous current. I opened my arms and let the robes spin away. I stopped turning and settled onto the light-dappled earth, expectant. A moment later, a loud "spang" resounded a few feet from my ear and a body fell face first onto my feet.

Chapter 18

I was in a car that seemed familiar, though not quite right. The car was moving. My weight shifted heavily as the car turned, shoving me against the arm rest on my right. My head bumped the window.

I looked at the driver: Skylar. She turned the steering wheel to the right, and I careened across the console to collide with her shoulder.

Straightening back up, I rubbed at my eyes. "Slow down."

"You're awake, good. Put on your seatbelt."

Fumbling to find the belt, I pulled it across me. "Hey, where are my clothes?"

"Back at Bryce's landscaping yard."

That didn't make sense. "Did you take off my clothes?"

"You took them off."

"Why would I do that? Why would I do that at a landscaping yard?"

"Hayley, sweetheart, you were being ravished."

"Ravished," I said to myself.

Someone was whimpering in the back seat. I turned and saw Jade huddled there. We stopped for a light. I sat back straight in my seat, looked out the window, and saw a gray-haired lady looking at me from another car. She stared. I slid lower in my seat.

I'd been at the landscaping yard, I remembered that. Everything had been dark and then light. Blue light had moved around me, swirling robes of light that I flung off. There was the sound of an impact. The weight falling onto me.

"You stopped him."

"Yes."

"He had a lot of magic. How did you find the magic to stop him?"

"Found it on the ground — the shovel I clobbered him with. You could say it was a magic shovel because it was magically lying exactly where I needed it."

"Say, I thought you were going to stay in the car and call the police if anything went wrong."

"That's what you told me to do. I guess you figured tonight was the night I was going to start letting you order me around. I don't know why you thought that. When I heard all the commotion from the yard — the blowers and chainsaws and whatnot — I thought you might need help quicker than the police could provide. That turned out to be correct."

Houses slipped past in a neighborhood I didn't recognize. Jade was still whimpering in the back seat. She pounded her fist on the back of my seat several times. I looked at the profile of Skylar's face in the dim light from the dashboard. "Thanks for saving me."

She looked back at me. Even in the dim light, her eyes told me she would have done anything to save me. We drove along in silence for a while. I began to realize that we weren't headed home.

"Where are we going?" I asked. "I want to go home."

"He knows where we live. He might follow us there. We can't take the chance."

She turned into the entrance of a Walmart and drove to the far side of the parking lot where no other cars were parked and the overhead light was out. It was exactly the kind of spot where we would never, ever park.

Skylar got out. "Get in the driver's seat, and if anybody approaches, drive away."

"I guess you're figuring I'm letting you order me around."

She gave me a *look*. Then, she did a shimmy down her body with her hands that said, "You wearing no clothes, girl."

I got in the driver's seat.

Half an hour later, I woke up when Skylar opened the door and I fell out of the car.

"Last time I leave you in charge of security," she said, shoving me upright. I struggled back to the passenger's side. She dropped a large shopping bag on the console between the seats and tossed another bag in the back seat.

When she was back in the car, she began pulling items of clothing out of the bag between the seats and handing them to me. Getting dressed in the car was a bother, but I was glad to have clothes again.

We spent the night in a motel near the Walmart. I slept fitfully. Jade startled us awake several times. Whenever I woke in the dark I felt completely lost. Skylar had to turn on the lights a few times to reassure me that everything was okay.

The last time I woke up, light was filtering through the curtains on the window. I replayed what had happened in my mind's eye for the twentieth time. Each time, I recalled more detail — scraping against the paving stones (I felt the clotted blood on my calf), the roaring of the machines, the incredible cascades of light. It was all terrifying, yet I wanted to be lifted up again by that light. I yearned to get that light back inside me. Gazing upward, I knew it was out there. I reached up to wipe away the haze that blocked the light. It didn't work. Puzzling. I wiped at it again.

"What do you see?"

I turned to find Skylar watching me from the other side of the bed. I let my arm drop. "It's what I don't see. I'm looking for that — the light."

After a while, I said, "You think it will get worse? I'll end up like Jade?"

"I think Jade's been ravished a lot. It probably gets worse the more times it happens. It's not going to happen again to you."

"That's good," I said wistfully. I still felt the pull of it down in my belly. "Who was it last night?"

Skylar raised onto one elbow to stare at me. "You mean you don't know? It was Bryce."

"But he's not magic. How could it be him? The magic was so powerful."

"He was wearing the ring. After I bashed him with the shovel, I saw the Bobcat's headlights glinting off the blue crystal. That must give him the power."

"Killin told me that whoever killed Lucan must be powerful, and he told me about the ring, but he didn't say the ring gave someone a lot of power — even to someone who's not magic."

"That was a glaring omission. Just about got you in trouble."

"Just about." I lifted my hand to wipe away the mist.

Skylar sighed and lay back onto her pillow. "The magic of that ring puzzles me," she said. "Could you tell me how you saw it, felt it?"

"And heard it. Well, the racket from all the yard equipment was obvious. I don't know if that was part of the magic. Sure was scary. But that was nothing compared to the eerie silence that came next."

"I heard the weed whackers and everything the whole time, so you must have gone into some kind of quiet bubble."

"You saw me rise into the air? Turn around? With light flowing around everything?"

"Just the headlights of the Bobcat. You stood next to that pile of flat stones and slowly rotated around on your tiptoes."

"Huh." I ran my fingers through my hair. "So it was all in my head."

"That's not saying it wasn't real."

I wasn't in the mood for a philosophical discussion about what's real and what's not. I looked to where Jade was asleep in the cot by the window. Whatever was real, she was really messed up. I didn't want to be like that.

"I want to talk to Killin," I said.

"I want to talk to Mother."

"Mother first."

Skylar's mother was in the middle of a spell to cure blossom end rot on her tomatoes, but she dropped everything when she heard what had happened. She raged for a minute about abuse of magic.

When her mother paused for breath, Skylar cut in, "How does ravishing work? How is it done?"

"Oh, sweetheart, I don't know how it works for the simple reason that I never wanted to know. That's twisted magic. You don't want to know how that works, trust me."

"Mother, Hayley's wellbeing might depend on knowing. The ravishing affected her in strange ways. Uh…" Skylar trailed off, looking at me with a question on her face.

"My memories…" I began, but I couldn't remember the problem with my memories. "Did Mary have a lamb?"

Skylar shook her head. "See?" she said to the phone.

"Oh dear, yes. When we talked about this before, I told you parts might be split off. I don't understand how that happens or exactly how it works. It's a side effect, you might say, of the intrusion. What I've heard is that the ravishing spell allows a man, usually a man, to penetrate another person's soul, usually a woman." She stopped abruptly and then continued. "It can also be physical. The bastard didn't do that, did he?"

"He was about to when I flattened part of his cranium with a shovel."

"Good girl. Whoever said that violence never solved anything?"

"I didn't see much room for negotiation at that particular moment," Skylar reflected. "The problem is, this guy is liable to come looking for us, and we can't count on always having a shovel handy. Do you know of any way to fend off the spell?"

"I don't know that it is a spell, as such. It might only be a power from an object, and I might have a spell to counter magic that's bound to an object. You said this ravishing guy isn't magic? He just has a ring that's magic?"

"So far as we know, he isn't magic. If he's the guy who killed Lucan Gunter, we could be wrong about him being magic."

"Let's hope the magic is all in the ring. I'll check on a defensive spell for that."

"If only we had a general-purpose defensive spell," Skylar said.

"If only 'if only' were magic," her mother replied, probably for the millionth time. "In the meantime, the best defense is to stay away from the guy with the ring."

"Will do. One other question before you go. If ravishing separates parts of the 'ravishee,' do you know any way to repair that?"

"I've heard of that problem from other causes, and they say it's possible to gather the parts. In ancient times, it was regarded as a quest, something akin to retrieving something from Hades or finding the Holy Grail. I'll check."

Skylar put down her phone and said to me, "So there's hope."

"And along the way we might find the Holy Grail," I said ruefully. "I think that was your mother's way of saying there's not much hope, which is mostly bad news for Jade. She's still breathing, isn't she?"

"Yeah, still going. After I clobbered Bryce and dragged you back to the car, she was pretty quiet. After a while, she started whimpering. I wonder if she's feeling his pain."

"You don't think she's linked to him, do you? Could he find us that way?"

Skylar didn't answer out loud. She gave me a dismayed look that was clear to read.

I put my hand on my head. "Do you think *I'm* linked to him?"

I wasn't going to lie there thinking about that. I got out of bed. "I'm taking a shower. Then, I'm going to go talk to Killin."

# # #

Skylar drove to the nursery, where I dashed in, tore off a few leaves of Tannis Beltane, and dashed out again without anyone seeing me. We ran the invisibility spell in shrubbery near the police station. Then, I spent an hour waiting for a chance to get to Killin's cell only to find he was no longer in it.

At that point, I was in the little corridor with four cells on it with no Killin to make a fuss so I could get out again. I had to haunt another man by tapping on the window of his cell door and talking to him through the grate about the precarious state of his pancreas until he began screaming for the guards to get him to the infirmary *now*. I probably scarred him for life. I am truly sorry, Stephen Rice. Hope your pancreas was okay.

When I was out of the jail and back with Skylar, she called the police station to see if we could visit Killin and was told that he had been moved to the L.A. County lockup. The person she talked to was nice enough to give her the phone number, so she quickly found out that we could talk to Killin during visiting hours, which were only half an hour away. No invisibility required.

I wasn't entirely visible when we got to the visitation center at the lockup, but who's really going to notice a detail like that?

"One of your eyes is missing," Killin said by way of greeting. "It's not a good look for you."

"Lovely to see you, too," I told him tartly.

"To be fair, it would be lovely to see you if I weren't looking straight through your skull. How did you get in here like that?"

"The guy who checked my photo ID didn't bat an eye at my missing eye."

We sadly wagged our heads over the lack of attentiveness in our public officials. I told him Skylar and I had found the man wearing the blue crystal ring. I told him what the man had done and what the man had tried to do.

Killin gripped the edge of the table between us. "I'll snap his noisome head off."

"Easy now," I said looking around. "Let's not talk about killing somebody when we're already in the slammer for killing somebody."

It was touching that he was livid on my account, but I hoped he wasn't the kind of man who went around killing people. We vegans are against that. Skylar was right: What kind of man was this who talked about wanting to kill Lucan Gunter? Now Bryce? I decided I'd better divert him to the bright side.

"The good news is that Skylar bashed him with a shovel."

"'Bashed him.' Could you be more specific?"

"Hit him in the head."

"How hard?"

"Killin, I don't know. Very hard."

"Was he still moving afterward?"

"Skylar said he was unconscious when she rolled him off of me, but he was starting to move again when she dragged me away."

"He was still moving?" His face flushed, and his eyes flashed. "So she didn't hit him hard enough."

"For which you should be grateful. Bryce probably killed Lucan, right? That's how he got Lucan's ring. With Bryce alive, we have a better chance of getting the police to nail him and let you go."

Killin nodded his head back and forth a couple of times in half-hearted agreement.

"Anyway, I'm fine, and by the way, you could have warned me about how powerful that ring is."

"You were in kind of a rush to get away, last time we chatted. The very next item out of my mouth was going to have been a note about that ring. It's got the ravishing power of a demon in it."

He squinted into the middle distance. "And you say that Skylar rescued you while this man was executing the ravishing? While the power of it was gathered around him? That's hard to credit."

"Why is that so unbelievable?" I asked him. "She's a brave, strong woman. She knows how to handle a shovel."

"It's not that," he said. "She could have a black belt in shovel fu, but if she was that close, the power of the ravishing would overcome her. You were eager to submit at that point, weren't you? That's what they say it's like. She'd get in line for him as well."

"Ah, well, it might have helped that she's a lesbian."

For the first time ever I saw him smile, a brief little smile, and just as quickly it turned to a frown. "Say, you're not, erm, you know…"

"Lesbian?" I asked helpfully.

He nodded faintly.

"I've been thinking about switching over. Men are too, how should I describe it? Lofty and condescending? That's part of it. Excessively violent? Distant and unavailable? Shall I go on?"

"Distant?" He threw up his hands. "I was pitching in your direction for all I was worth from the first moment I walked into your place of business and saw you standing at the counter."

My jaw literally fell open at this bit of news. That aloof, condescending air? That was his pitch? I tapped my fingernail distractedly on the table between us. "In any case," I said, "our visiting time is short, and I'm wondering if you know of any way to repair the damage done by ravishing."

He rapped the table with his knuckles, made a gesture with his open hand that said *of course*, and nodded to himself. "The Ullswater mason."

"I should know about this?"

"I should have understood this sooner. You're the stone walker who was foretold, and with the help of the Ullswater mason, you can find the path to retrieve the parts of the soul lost to ravishing. It's obvious. It was always happening this way."

"You've lost me."

"Let me tell you the story of the ring with the blue crystal — as much as I know of it."

"How about only as much as we have time for?" I asked, glancing at the clock on the wall.

But he was already leaning back in his plastic chair, gazing at the far corner of the ceiling. "That ring was originally forged in Samaria. It's covered in Cuneiform script, the earliest form of writing. Looks like little marks made by chickens."

He looked at me and said, "You've seen this writing? The script on the ring says something about how much one person owes another, which is code for a magic spell. Archeologists have found lots of these scripts and never figured out what's really going on. Anyway, the ring was brought to England many centuries ago. It was thrown into a beck that flows into the Ullswater."

"Wait. What's a beck? And why would anyone throw a ring into one? For that matter, what's the Ullswater?"

"The Ullswater is a lake in the English Lake District, where a stream is known as a beck. The ring was thrown into the beck to rouse the witch of the Westmoreland by a knight who was mortally wounded, probably in Arthur's time. The witch healed the man's wounds, saved his life. The ring then passed from the witch to various other magical people, one of whom combined it with a couple of different magical objects. One of those objects was a scepter, but I'm unclear about what happened with all that. Eventually, the ring was separated again, and its magic was bent by a demonic fellow near Castlerigg to cast the ravishing spell."

"Which means?" I looked at the clock pointedly.

"Which means the ring's magic is tied to the Ullswater Stoneway, which I won't try to explain now. Suffice it to say that you have appeared at this moment in history to walk the Stoneway." He held his hands palms up to indicate *this is obvious*.

I drummed my fingernails on the table a few times. "I'm not really into the whole destiny thing," I told him.

"Destiny doesn't care if you're into it. What matters is whether it has a path laid out for you."

I waggled my head back and forth. "Yes, yes, Obi Wan, it is my destiny."

"That was Darth Vader's line. And, okay, it does sound melodramatic. But you know how people like to say that their fates aren't set in stone? In this case, they are. Yours is. Set in stone, that is."

# # #

Destiny, fate, whatever. Killin assured me that if I followed his directions, I'd be able to retrieve the wandering parts of ravished souls. That included my own unstuck parts, as well as Jade's and Bryce's, which started me thinking about a plan for resolving this whole mess.

Chapter 19

Out the window over Greenland, I saw far below me an endless expanse of ice reflecting moonlight. What if Killin had told me I needed to go there? I shivered. He'd sent me a long way from home to what seemed like the ends of the earth, but at least I didn't have to get all frozen in ice. The endless ice was beautiful in the moon glow, but what if I could talk to ice rather than stone?

I was smiling to myself, thinking how easy I had it, when turbulence jolted the plane sideways. We fell for several seconds and then shuddered upward. Every tray table and overhead bin in the cabin rattled like it was going to come unhinged. The other passengers woke, gasping in alarm, and the captain turned on the fasten seatbelt sign. We lurched around the sky. Babies cried. Grownups murmured to one another.

I'm not a particularly anxious flyer, but I was wishing I believed in fate. If I were destined to walk the Ullswater Stoneway, then I would not perish by crashing into the Greenland ice sheet. I and everyone else on this plane would land safely at Heathrow.

Or would we? What if my fate was indeed set in stone, and Killin was wrong about what was set? What if it was my destiny to fall out of the sky over Greenland? I looked out the window and saw only black darkness. We were past Greenland. My destiny was not there. How about the North Sea? Not better, really.

My life could be following a narrow course chiseled in stone, like a wheel set in a groove, and if I couldn't see the groove, what difference did it make? Then again, what if I could see the groove? What if I walked the Stoneway and saw my fate? Knowing everything about my course in life sounded like a bore.

For sure, it would be nice to have a few certainties in life. I'd like to know what Killin was all about. Could I trust him? I'd like to know who killed Lucan Gunter. I'd like to know what happened to my mother. Well, that was in the past. That was all in the past. How could I ever know the future when so much of my past was missing?

I looked out the window again and saw only a complete black blank. I tried to wipe off the window to clear it. Then I slumped back in the seat. I was trying to see through to the absent light, my missing parts, my supposed destiny. At least the turbulence had eased. People around me were nodding off.

Up and down, back and forth. The course of my life was all over the place. Even if it was a path set in stone, what of it? Knowing a course doesn't clarify everything. I knew that the shortest path from L.A. to London was over Greenland. I got on this plane at LAX, I passed over Greenland, and I'd get off at Heathrow. It didn't quite make sense to me, but there it was. Maybe it was magic.

# # #

I'd never driven a Land Rover before. As I sped up the M40 from Heathrow Airport, I thought I might be able to get used to the leather seats and butt-kicking power. Killin had recommended I rent one of these beasts because he wasn't entirely clear where I might need to go in the wilder parts of the Lake District.

After five hours of driving under threatening skies and light rain squalls, I pulled into Penrith, a few miles north of the Ullswater. The skies now made good their threats by releasing apocalyptic quantities of rain. I drove slowly through the downpour to my bed and breakfast, thankful for GPS. After waiting in the Land Rover for a few minutes, hoping this was a cloudburst that would quickly pass, I dashed for the front door. The first ten feet soaked me, and I really looked forward to going for a long hike in *this* weather.

The next morning the rain was still teeming down. After breakfast, I went to a shop on the high street and bought a good raincoat. The shop next door sold me a proper pair of boots.

Killin had told me to hike up a track that ran along the Aira Beck. The track was rocks and mud and sand and rocks and mud. It ran by a couple of waterfalls that would have been beautiful in sunlight. On this day, everything was soggy and cold, yet I met a lot of people on the trail. Brits didn't seem to think anything of slogging about in the rain and being cheerful about it into the bargain. Sheep with fuzzy white lambs grazed on the rolling green hillsides.

After a couple of miles, the path branched. I took the narrower left-hand path. In the next mile or so, I didn't pass any other hikers. Eventually, I came to a cairn of smooth stones followed by an outcropping of gray rock that resembled a horse's head. At least, that's the way Killin had described it. It looked more like the head of a tyrannosaurus. I took the path anyway.

A mile later, a stone cottage appeared next to an overhang of rock that had a stream cascading down one side of it. The stream disappeared into the ground after it fell over the face of the overhang.

The cottage was made of rectangular stones that were cut more or less square at the corners of the building and irregular in the rest of the walls. One corner of the ancient structure sagged. The stones wore dark gray splotches of faintly green lichen. Patches of moss grew in the cracks. The stonework was all dark with rain. The single window on the front had four panes, one of them filled in with a piece of slate. Water dripped off every surface, and a few yards away the stream splashed loudly.

I knocked on the cottage's wooden door. The sodden oak planks were so thick I could scarcely hear my own knock. I banged harder with the heel of my hand and waited. Water dripped off the slate roof onto the hood of my raincoat. No one came to the door. I banged harder and went to peer in the uncurtained window.

The room was mostly dark. A low fire burned in the fireplace, which was made of the same gray stone as the outside walls of the cottage. A dim light in the far corner of the room came from a lamp with a yellow flame inside a glass chimney.

Peering through the clouded windowpane, I began to make out the face of a very large man sitting in the corner. His deeply lined face was framed by cascades of wild, violently red hair going to gray and a long wiry red beard. The man's mouth was open and the face contorted horribly. A huge hairy hand came up and wiped at the man's eyes. He glanced toward the window then, jerked his head up, and his eyes widened. Then, he leapt out of his chair.

The man was stupendously big.

Stumbling back a couple of steps from the window, I turned to run. Wrong place! I'd found the giant from the fairytales!

As I high-tailed it down the path, the giant threw his front door open and yelled, "Stop!"

I wasn't about to stop.

"Stop, damn it!"

I definitely wasn't about to stop damn it. Running wasn't easy in my new boots, but I figured I could outpace a giant so long as I kept going full tilt.

He hadn't shouted at me for a few seconds, so I looked around to see where he was and was shocked to find him only a few yards behind me. That's when I hit a slick patch of mud, slid over a lip of rock, and plunged into a pool of deep, cold water. Frigidly cold water. My body compressed into a slender sliver of shuddering flesh, trying to escape the cold that pressed from all sides like jamming into the Greenland ice sheet with a giant after me.

I came up gasping for breath.

The giant was on me in a second. He grabbed my arm with his hairy paw. Reaching desperately around the edge of the pool, I found a grapefruit-sized rock and swung at his jaw with all my might. He deflected my hand with his other paw. The giant yanked me half out of the pool and laid me down hard on a flat rock. We were both panting.

I struggled to get to my feet, pulling against the grip on my arm. He hissed in my face through broken teeth, "I've been waiting for you for 386 years. I'm not letting you get away now."

He dragged me the rest of the way out of the pool.

"Let's go inside and get these wet things off," he growled.

When he pulled me to my feet with a grunt, he towered over me. He looked to be about eight feet tall and broad as a door. I kicked him in the shin, hard, and turned to run. He grabbed the day pack I was wearing and snatched me backward.

"Damn it!" he shouted. "Would you stop for one moment? I'm the one you came to see."

"Who are you?" I yelled, though I didn't really care at that point. I was facing away from him and trying to yank free from his grip.

"I'm the Ullswater Mason!" he bellowed.

"Why are you chasing me?" I yelled back.

"Because you're running away. Just. Be. Still!" He released his grip on my pack at the same instant I found the buckle that held it on.

I stumbled forward a few steps while the pack slid to the ground behind me. I looked over my shoulder at the giant and my pack on the ground between us. The pack had my wallet in it, my passport.

"For one moment. Please," the giant pleaded.

He sat heavily on a boulder and rubbed his shin. I edged a few yards further away and eyed him. He was one scary dude. Maybe I could get along okay without my wallet and passport.

"Look," he said, "I apologize for chasing you. When a man waits several centuries for a prophecy to be fulfilled, and the big day finally arrives, he gets overexcited, you understand?"

"Sure," I told him. "I get overexcited waiting a few days for a package to arrive, never mind centuries." Another destiny merchant was all I needed, and like I was going to believe this story about waiting 386 years.

"You're the stonewalker," he said. "I've been seeing signs that you would arrive soon. I need to instruct you in following the way, kenning the pattern. We need to begin preparing right away."

"I'm freezing right now," I told him. My teeth were starting to chatter. I'd been chilled even before I fell into the pool of water. "I need to go find a warm place. I'll come back another day."

"No!" He made a move to stop me, and I backed away as quickly as I could with my boots sloshing water. "I'll stoke the fire. You'll warm up quickly here. It's miles back down the hill. Please don't chance it."

He was right. I was shivering, though whether from the cold or from the idea of going in that little cottage with this rough giant, I wasn't sure. A violent shiver shook me as I looked at him. I nodded. He snagged my pack with one finger, turned, and ran up the path. I slogged behind him as quickly as I could.

The front door of the cottage stood open. The giant squatted in front of the fire waving his huge hands slowly back and forth. Fire magic. The flames leapt up, roaring. I could feel the heat from the open doorway. The warmth was irresistible. Scary giant or no, I was going to get by that fire.

The giant stood aside as I plodded in and fell to my knees on the hearth. I stripped off my raincoat. Soon my sodden clothes were steaming. I turned around to warm my back. The giant was standing by the front window, shivering, letting me have the heat. I motioned for him to come beside me in front of the fire.

The giant had dropped my pack by the front door. On the off chance that my phone hadn't drowned when I fell into the pool, I fished it out of a supposedly waterproof pocket and laid it by the fireplace to dry.

When both sides of me had warmed a little, I sat down, got my boots off, and held my feet to the fire. The giant did the same. I don't remember fairytales mentioning the odor of giants' feet, but they should include that little detail. When you're in a little room with a wet giant, the smell gradually becomes the second most important detail.

The number one important detail was this: What was this creature going to do with me? Not a detail, really. Killin had obviously warned the giant that I was coming. I wasn't entirely sure of Killin's motives, so I was even less sure of the giant's.

This whole setup seemed like an elaborate trap, except that I hardly felt like I was worth building an elaborate trap for. Why not just waylay me in Redondo Beach? Why get me way out here? Unless this was a scheme to deliver fresh meat to the giant. I eyed the man next to me in the dark blue overalls. Was he going to grind my bones to make his bread?

As remote as this place was, the giant surely had easier ways to get groceries than having them shipped over from America. Killin and the giant wanted me to do something for them, something that required talking with rocks. They wanted to find out something? No harm in that. Change something? That posed more of a problem.

What could they want to change that had to do with rocks? I racked my brain for clues. I reached into the air and tried to wipe away the obstructions. I hardly knew anything. Why hadn't I asked Killin more about what he was after? So much was unknown.

Sitting on the hearth, I looked out the window at a craggy gray mountain peak that emerged briefly from a rain squall and disappeared again behind a swirling curtain of mist and rain. Hail pinged off the window glass and pounded dully on the roof and just as suddenly stopped. A ray of sunlight swept across the mountain, illuminating its green flanks and lingering for a moment on the broken gray rock at the summit.

How could any of this be real? I'd followed a winding path up from the Ullswater. The path led by waterfalls and clear pools. I'd come around bends in this muddy track and found lambs huddled under their mothers. I'd taken a less-traveled branch of the path and now sat by the hearth of a stone cottage with a giant. None of this made sense.

I thought of what Skylar had told me again and again: If it made sense, it wouldn't be magic. I turned sideways to the fire and glanced at the giant. I was in a fairytale. It was never going to make sense. I was never going to figure it out. The only way to know where the path led was to follow it around the bend and see what was there.

"Killin wasn't clear about what I would do here," I told the giant. I turned my back to the fire.

"Bardis? That rogue's never been clear about anything in his life."

The giant got up off his knees and walked to the window. "I knew his mother. A free spirit, she was. Didn't raise him right. That's what her people in County Wicklow told me. Let him go about as he pleased from the first day he could walk on his own two feet. People in the village were always bringing him home from wherever he'd wandered, and she'd say only *thanks* and ask the child what he'd seen."

He turned from the window and regarded me. "You're not involved with him, are you? Killin Bardis?"

I stared back at him, a little puzzled. "He sent me. You know that."

The giant's brow furrowed. "I do?"

This act was not going to fool me. "You knew I talked to rocks as soon as you saw me. There's only one way you could know that, and his name is Killin Bardis."

He shook his head. "I can see it, the Stoneway connection. I was trained to see it in someone who can walk the Stoneway. It's why I'm here. It's why I'm the Ullswater Mason. I can't walk the

Stoneway myself, but I see that you can. I see it as a fire in you like molten rock burning in the earth. I don't need the likes of Killin Bardis to tell me anything about that.

"Say, that's why you were so afraid." He grinned, his broken teeth jagged across the width of his enormous mouth. "You were sent here by a man who's not to be trusted, so you didn't trust me. But if that's the case, why did you come here at all?"

I told him about the murder and how Killin had been arrested for it. "Since then, I've become pretty sure that the perp is another man, and I'm trying to prove that Killin is not the murderer."

"Well now, he may be a rascal, but I can't believe he'd perp somebody."

"Perp means —" I started, but I could tell by the giant's expression that he knew perfectly well what perp means. I didn't tell him that Killin had confessed that he *intended* to kill Lucan Gunter. Anyway, that wasn't the same as killing somebody. What kind of rascal was Killin? I'd have to find out some other time. The fire had warmed me just about enough to trudge back down the mountain.

"My name is Hayley," I said to the giant, extending my hand.

"Bowl," he said, stepping toward the fire to take my little hand gently in his giant one.

"Pleased to meet you," I said. "Bowl?"

"Played cricket ages ago. I was a champion bowler in my time. That means —" He saw my expression and stopped. "You know that's like a pitcher in baseball."

"My father was a cricketer, when he wasn't playing polo or shooting at something."

I got to my feet. "Well, Bowl, I'm going to go back to my B&B and soak in a tub of hot water for the rest of the day. I'll come back up tomorrow morning, and you can show me how to walk the Stoneway?"

He looked horrified. "You can't leave! You have to begin instruction. I built a room at the back you can stay in while you train. You don't want to waste time going up and down the mountain."

"You want me to stay overnight?" I looked around the ancient cottage and pictured myself sleeping in a stone cell next to this giant. "I don't mind going up and down the mountain. I like to walk. It will give me time to absorb what I need to learn. How long does this take, anyway?"

"Months, many months, and that's if you stay and focus completely on the Stoneway." He held out his hands imploringly. "The Stoneway is like a Celtic knot done in stone. Branches of the path pass under and through other parts that must be walked *through* the stone. The Stoneway composes the order of the earth, the framework of time across human affairs. Its influence extends to every aspect of life. You have to dedicate yourself to it."

"Months?"

No way was I going to stay up here that long. If that's how long the Stoneway took, my plan to put Bryce behind bars and free Killin wasn't going to work. I couldn't retrieve Jade's scattered parts. Or my own. I picked up my phone and turned it on. It lit up but got no signal.

It wasn't my destiny to walk the Stoneway. Whenever could I possibly take months out of my life to come stay with this giant in a stone hut? And for what? The only reason I was ever interested in the Stoneway was to untangle the mess around the murder.

As I walked out the door of the cottage, I muttered, "Sorry," to Bowl. I put on my raincoat, though the rain had finally stopped.

He shouted after me, "You were born to walk the Stoneway. I can see it in you. Please come back. You must come back. You're betraying everyone."

I kept walking. I didn't have time to do something for everyone. I had to do something for a few people I cared about right away.

"You're failing us! You're failing every single person." He paused for a breath. Then he bellowed, "You're failing yourself!"

My damp clothes were chafing me at every step, and when I reached the branch in the path, the skies opened with a punishment of rain.

Chapter 20

The Land Rover had a heated seat. In a couple of minutes, the world was made glorious again. I congratulated myself on ditching the destiny that everybody else thought was mine. I had nearly a full tank of gas and could go anywhere I wanted.

Sitting in the Land Rover by the Aira Beck, that glorious feeling lasted a minute or two. Where did I want to go? The short-term answer was clear: to Penrith, to the B&B. Then home. I put the car in gear and drove out of the parking lot, up the road that ran along the Ullswater.

On the Land Rover's satellite radio I found an oldies channel. I could hear the same old tunes anywhere in the world. Annoyingly, "The Long and Winding Road" came on. I turned the radio off and drove in silence for a while. The wet road hissed under my tires, rain drummed on the roof, the wipers pumped back and forth. Was I doing the right thing? I turned the radio back on in time to hear McCartney sing "Don't leave me waiting here" and punched the off button. I was doing the right thing. I told myself that several times in a commanding voice.

At the B&B, I drew a tub of hot water and lowered my aching body into it gratefully. The world was glorious yet again. Left alone with my own thoughts and nothing else to do, I got out again five minutes later. It was too early to eat dinner, and anyway, I wasn't hungry. I said goodbye to the nice couple who ran the B&B, and pointed the Land Rover south through the rain toward London.

Six hours later, I returned the Land Rover at the airport and went to the British Airways desk to change my flight to the next available one that would take me toward home. The woman behind the counter told me I could get a flight to San Francisco in three hours and then get a shuttle to L.A. Perfect.

When she asked for my passport, I looked at her dumfounded. I can only imagine that she thought me a complete idiot, because I must have had a look on my face that seemed to say that I had no idea what a passport was.

What my look was actually saying was this, and I quote exactly: My passport is in a day pack in the stone cottage of Bowl the giant.

I thought about saying this out loud to the British Airways woman to confirm that I was a nut job, in case she had any doubts, but I only said, "Never mind," and walked away from the desk rolling my little carry-on bag. I had no ID. I couldn't fly, and I couldn't rent another car to drive back to the Ullswater. I stood in the middle of the terminal and considered crying. That was something I could do without an ID.

My father had always told me when I traveled to keep a credit card and some cash separate from my other stuff in case of emergency. Throughout my younger years, I'd steadfastly ignored everything my father told me. I did not have a credit card I kept separate for emergencies — yet another fact I didn't want to think about. These sorts of facts were piling up around me there in the Heathrow terminal.

After standing briefly in the middle of the terminal not crying, I sat down for a while and managed to continue not crying. I put my hand into the air to wipe away everything that troubled me, to try to see my missing parts. Finally, I thought through several facts that I'd been avoiding with the expectation they would make me cry, which they did, but only a little. My destiny was reaching out tiny clutching fingers that plucked at my clothing, tugging at me, pulling me where I did not want to go.

I called Skylar and woke her from a sound sleep. Between us, we came up with a plan. I had enough change in my pocket to ride the tube from the airport to a train station in London, where Skylar called in her credit card number to a travel agent who provided a train ticket. This ticket took me directly to Penrith faster than I could have driven there.

Arriving in Penrith around midmorning, I walked the two miles from the train station to the B&B where I'd stayed. The couple who ran the place were happy to see me. Wide-eyed, they told me that a giant had knocked on their door just after I'd left the day before and told them he had something that belonged to me.

When they told him I'd left to go home, he frowned and then broke out in a ghastly grin.

"His teeth were all jagged," the woman said.

"But he seemed a nice enough bloke," the man added.

Bowl told them I'd be back. They were so impressed that I knew this giant, they were delighted to drive me the ten miles along the lake to where the Aira Beck tumbled down.

The rain had cleared, and today the Aira Force waterfalls were sparkling in the sunlight. Lambs darted and twirled a few feet from their mothers on the green hillsides. Song birds sang. A farmer with a handsome border collie said, "Good day to you, lass."

In short, the world was glorious. It was all perfectly annoying. I kicked several loose stones as I walked, sending them careening into the Aira Beck. I was going to march into Bowl's cottage, grab my pack, and march straight back down this hill. After that, I could get an Uber to Penrith and catch the train back to London. That was my plan for the day.

Bowl was sitting in the doorway of his cottage. He grinned his jagged smile when he saw me and waved cheerfully. "Glorious day, isn't it?"

"Glorious," I conceded. "Bowl, thanks for trying to return my pack."

"You are most welcome. My apologies for snooping inside so I could find out where you were. Or had been."

"How did you get all the way to Penrith?"

"Callum Gunn, local farmer. He carries me to town with him sometimes, when he goes."

"That's nice of him. Look, Bowl, I can't take time to do the training for the Stoneway right now. I just can't. I'm sorry. Maybe someday."

"Would you have a few minutes to talk about it? Then, you'll know a bit about the Stoneway and how it relates to you. At least have a cup of tea before you tramp back down the hill." He stood up and went inside without waiting for an answer. I followed.

He ran water from a tap into an electric kettle and started it heating.

"You have running water and electricity?" I asked.

"The water is piped from an uphill spring, and the creek drives a small generator. I put in that generator back in the 1920s."

"You can't possibly be that old," I said before I could stop myself.

Bowl gave me a patient frown. "I'm much older than that. You don't understand yet. Let me tell you about the Stoneway. Please sit." He gestured toward a wooden chair at his small table.

He turned back to the tea canister and said, "A long time ago — I don't know how long, but much more than a thousand years — a sorcerer and a witch decided that the world had seen just about enough violence. This pair had powerful magic. They used their magic to set patterns in stone that could influence human behavior in a more peaceful direction. Some patterns set out models for working toward agreement without drawing swords. Other patterns were more expansive and sought to draw the human imagination toward cooperation."

Standing on the opposite side of the table from me, he said, "The catch is that the Stoneway must be maintained. Its patterns break in earthquakes, and its power runs down like a battery, you might say, and needs to be recharged. That requires a stonewalker." He looked pointedly at me.

"All right," I told him, thinking that this all sounded preposterous. I mean, who's noticed that the world has been peaceful in the past thousand years? "How often does this recharge need to be done? Do we have a few years?"

"We are now a little more than a century overdue." The water had come to a boil. He poured it into the teapot. "The world wars should never have happened. And I know what you're thinking. The world has rarely gone without wars, so the Stoneway must not be much good anyway. Trust me when I say that human affairs would be much worse without the Stoneway, and they will continue to get worse until a stonewalker brings new magic."

"But why has it been so long? Why wasn't the thing recharged a century ago?"

"We get precious few stonewalkers. If one fails to appear, or simply refuses, it is a long wait until another comes along."

Bowl set the teapot on the table and brought a cup and saucer for each of us. Sitting down at the other side of the table, he gazed at me thoughtfully. "I can see you there, thinking that after all this time, a few more months, a few more years, won't hurt anything. Think on it, Hayley. What if something happens to you in the meantime? For that matter," he said, getting up again, "what if something happens to me?"

He went to an alcove in the wall and brought back an elegant China creamer. "You prefer cow's milk, I presume?"

"I prefer my tea straight up, actually."

He poured the tea and sat down. "As I mentioned yesterday, I've been waiting 386 years for you to arrive, and the magic that keeps me alive is waning. If I finally take my last breath without a replacement, it doesn't matter how many stonewalkers arrive at my door."

I imagined arriving at the giant's cottage and finding it empty. That would be a lot less scary. It would also be tragic if I believed what he was telling me. Did I believe? Could this giant be centuries old? Was I a fabled stonewalker, fated to walk the ancient Stoneway?

One lesson I'd learned from living in California was that most amazing stories were just talk. On the other hand, I'd learned that some stories — often the most outlandish — turn out to be true.

While thinking all this, I took a sip of tea and practically choked. It was the strongest, bitterest tea I'd ever put in my mouth.

"Proper English tea," Bowl pointed out. He nudged the creamer my way with his huge finger.

I didn't feel like explaining the vegan thing. I got up and poured half my tea in the sink and thinned out the half that was left with water from the electric kettle. "Even if I believe all this about the Stoneway, I can't take months to do it now. Killin is in jail for a murder he didn't commit, and the actual perp is a menace. He has a ring that belonged to Lucan Gunter. He's using the power of that ring to ravish my friend Jade, and he could be using that power on other people as well. Me, for instance." I sipped my tea. It was still a bit strong.

"The ring with the blue crystal? I've been hoping to get that back. It was linked to this place ages ago. Has a lot of power. It would keep me going for another century."

"If I can get it from the guy who's wearing it, I'll be happy to bring it to you. In the meantime, the ravishing has left my friend and me with parts scattered and missing. My friend is in bad shape. Killin tells me that I can use the Stoneway to retrieve our missing parts."

"No, no! I told you he's a rogue. You don't *use* the Stoneway."

"So it's not possible? I've come all this way for nothing?"

"Not for nothing! You can walk the Stoneway! You can save the world!"

"Save the world, uh-huh. I can't save a couple of people I care about, but I can save the world. You know, Bowl, my friend, this is all a bit over the top."

"In the fullness of time," he said, "you will come to understand."

I put my cup down. "I can't wait around for time to get full. I'll have to go with half a tank."

Standing up from the table, I told Bowl without looking at him, "Sorry to get your hopes up. I'll just grab my stuff and get along down the mountain. I need to go find a plan B. Thanks for the tea." I went past him to lift my pack from the wooden peg it was hanging on.

He put his hand on my arm. "Wait," he said. "It is possible to retrieve parts in the Stoneway, but it's horribly dangerous. It would take you on far flung paths that twist and branch endlessly. Even with a strong beacon at your starting point, you would probably be unable to return. Your body would be left clutching rock, while your *self* wanders forever in the earth. It would be a living hell. You would not save your friend or anything else."

"So it *is* possible," I said.

He stared for a second. Then he went off on me, ranting about young people today, impossible to talk sense, think they know everything, and numerous other topics. I'd heard it all before. When he finally calmed down, I asked him what I needed to do to retrieve stray parts. He told me I couldn't because I needed a stone with the person's imprint on it, which was the only way to find and contain that person's parts. I told him I had the stone. Killin had already explained that much.

Bowl told me to go away and come back in the morning. He would think about it overnight. With that he ushered me out and slammed the door behind me.

I Ubered to Penrith and rented another car, this one a lot less impressive than the Land Rover. Then, I was at loose ends for the rest of the day. I walked. I rode across the Ullswater on a little steam-powered ferryboat. I hid a credit card in a safe place for future emergencies.

The next morning, with the sun obscured by low-hanging mist, I hiked up along the Aira Beck. I was carrying a stone with Jade's imprint as well as one of the paving stones from Bryce's landscaping yard, which was getting very heavy by the time I got to Bowl's cottage.

When he answered my knock, he said, "I will tell you how to retrieve parts if you swear to me you will return within a year to walk the Stoneway. That's if you survive the retrieval, of course. Do you swear?"

I held up my hand and said, "I do solemnly swear."

He led me up the slope behind his cottage and around a shallow pool in the rock. We stopped at an overhang of rock that created a sheltered spot beneath it.

"The Stoneway exists everywhere and nowhere in the rocky substance of the earth. Gateways such as this one make it easier to access."

"Should I take off my clothes so I can get my body against the rock?"

He gave me a perplexed look. "If you want to die of exposure while you lose yourself in the stone, love, feel free to strip off."

"I think I won't."

"When you're trained to walk the Stoneway, you'll be able to meld your body right into the stone. That's a much safer approach. As it is, you'll be lying here for many hours." He lay a wool blanket down on the broken rock under the overhang.

I took off my heavy pack and set it down next to the blanket. "Melding into the rock is safer? I don't get that."

He put his hands on his hips and shook his head. "That's because you haven't grasped the difficulty here."

"Which is?"

"Finding your way back. You'll be ranging across the entire earth by diverse paths. If you take your body with you, you can emerge from the Stoneway through any gateway, any time you become disoriented. Doing this now, without proper training, you'll have to find your way back to this place, come what may." He stamped his boot on the rock.

He could stamp on rock all he wanted. I was not afraid. I'd found my way through stone before. I could see my way clear to do this. I looked up beyond the overhang of rock and reached out to wipe clear the mist that obscured my vision. I yanked my hand out of the air in exasperation.

"Let's get on with it," I told him. I sat down on the blanket.

"Find a comfortable position where you can hold one hand against this outcrop of rock and your other hand on the rock that has your friend's imprint."

"I have three rocks for three people, actually. How should I do that?"

"You should not do that. I thought you had one friend who was ravished. Who are these other people?"

Taking two rounded river rocks out of my pack, I held them up. "Besides my friend Jade, I have my friend Skylar, who was ravished in a dream the same way I was the first time. I don't think we lost many parts that time, so it's not a big deal. Don't worry about that one. The other person," I said, heaving the paving stone out of my pack, "is the guy who did all the ravishing. He seems to have lost a lot of parts himself."

"You want to retrieve the parts of the man who ravished you? Why would you even want to do that?"

"Because I have to, that's all." I was getting impatient with all this talk.

Bowl tapped his giant foot on the rock several times. "All right. It would be safer to fetch the parts for one person at a time. You don't give a fig for safety, so put your hand on all the stones and have a go at it."

I put the Jade and Skylar stones under my palm and the Bryce stone under my fingertips. I reached out and found a place on the rock in front of me where I could rest my other hand.

"Now you need to create a beacon so you can find your way back to this spot. The simplest way is to shout your name three times while you focus on the feel of the rock in your hands."

"Hayley West," I shouted three times, feeling a little silly.

"Even though you are not properly trained, and entirely against my better judgment, I'm going to tell you the key to the Stoneway. You are not to abuse it. Do you understand?"

I nodded. I had no idea what abusing it would look like, but I didn't want to get bogged down in unnecessary detail.

Bowl began chanting meaningless stuff that started with "Elberith gothanigal woll stot. Piconah anah…"

It took me a few minutes to learn this mess.

"To find the parts you want, call the name of the person into the Stoneway or cast impressions of the person. Begin by retrieving your own parts. That will make it easier to do everything else. Ready?"

I nodded.

"Hayley, if anything goes wrong, I'll try to bring you back from the dead."

"You can actually do this? You've done it before?"

"Twice. Well, once, if you count the times it actually worked. The other one was a zombie. I didn't have the proper newt to get the job done. It's a rare bugger."

"So you'll be trading a newt's life for mine? A rare one at that?"

"If you need another reason to return safely, there you have it. Otherwise, perhaps you can live with it."

"So to speak. And can you actually get the proper newt this time?"

Bowl reached into the pocket of his overalls and removed a small mason jar in which a red newt was swimming. "I'm ready."

Turning to the stone, I took a deep breath. "I'm ready too." I began chanting the key to the Stoneway.

Immediately, I felt myself lurch into the rock face with tremendous force. A tornado of wind tore at my skin and squeezed me. Then, a loud bang resounded right behind me and propelled me forward like a rocket. The stone path opened up, veered to the left, and branched a dozen times before I could notice where I was or recognize any landmarks to help me get back to where I started. I was lost and flailing in the first five seconds as an unseen force thrust me forward past glass cubes full of spheres and spheres full of cubes, followed by a blur of bookshelves that seemed to go on forever in all directions. I hurtled along, completely out of control. Bowl was right. This was crazy.

Chapter 21

Plunging, lunging, and swooping this way and that, I tried to relax so I could think straight. I'd been flying through the Stoneway for half an hour, swerving around hairpin turns, looping crossways through narrow fissures, even flipping end over end after skidding down a transparent chute that seemed to be made of ice. I went by a chicken made of paper, some kind of spindly machinery, and a series of green fire hydrants before passing through a forest of giant purple ferns.

None of it seemed entirely real. The objects and structures all looked as though someone had constructed them. They lacked the detail of real-world stuff, or they were ever so slightly translucent, or they were the wrong color.

Try as I might, I couldn't exert a bit of control over my travel, and I didn't have the slightest notion where I was. I kept telling myself to not panic, relax, relax. The transparent chute got me thinking that all my movement was like skating on ice, and I thought that if only I were rollerblading, I could put on the brakes. Instantly, I felt like I was rollerblading, so I tilted my foot to brake.

Gradually, I slowed and came to a stop in the corridor of an old office building. At least, that's what it looked like. The floor was scuffed lavender-tinged wood, and I could see doors on either side of the hallway stretching forever in front of me. Some of the doors were open. I looked behind me and saw a similar series of office doors curving away into the distance. It was perfectly quiet and dusty, as if it had been abandoned for a long time.

I bladed through one of the open doors and found myself in a grove of blooming pink trees. Cherry blossoms were falling around me, making a clinking sound as they sprinkled onto the ground. I turned and rolled slowly back through the space where the doorway had been. The snow of blossoms abruptly stopped. I was now in a narrow valley created by enormous folds of azure blue fabric.

The paths here weren't logical. As with all magic, the Stoneway didn't make sense in any conventional way. I needed magic to guide me.

Remembering what Bowl had told me, I called out my name. If only I were in a car, I could drive around to collect my scattered parts. My body shifted into a sitting posture, and I began speeding along, drawn to something I couldn't see.

How far could I push the as-if magic? I pressed my foot on an invisible accelerator pedal and went faster, flashing past all manner of odd objects. I called out my name periodically and let myself be drawn forward. After an hour or so, I began circling a series of multicolored fragments hanging in the air. They looked like shards of glass, scraps of paper, autumn leaves that glittered. I called out my name to them. They clung to the sound of my voice and swirled in a whirlwind around my body. As they disappeared into me, I saw flashes of my life — fried chicken at a friend's house, a new Barbie dress, part of a biochemistry lecture (if only I'd gotten this reminder during the final for that course), several movies that were hardly worth remembering. I could have done without remembering the girl who attacked me in high school or the horse that threw me when I was 13. But I was glad to get back the memory of a freckle-faced boy named Anthony who kissed me during a creepy movie about giant insects.

With the memory of my first kiss restored, I called my name again and moved on. For another hour, I drove around, collecting my parts — many dozens of them scattered all over the place. Oddly, none were of my mother. Most were banal and many others better forgotten. My memory was a junkyard.

The last place I was drawn to was a complete surprise. It looked like the backyard of a house I knew very well. I'd grown up in this rambling white house in Connecticut. I knew every tree, and shrub, and granite statue on the sprawling grounds. Standing at the edge of a pond surrounded by massive oaks and boulders left by glaciers, I felt like a little girl again.

The place was hauntingly familiar, except that most of it was a different color than it should be. This place also differed in one other detail: On a little island in the pond was a stone plinth that never existed in the real world. On that carved stone was a glittering transparent sphere about the size of a beach ball. Three triangular shards spun slowly inside, throwing off every color of the rainbow.

Unlike the other parts I'd collected, these had animated scenes glowing on their surfaces. They seemed to be both calling to me and warning me away. I waded into the water and found that it only came to my knees.

When I reached the stone plinth, I laid my hands on its cold surface. Impressions from the parts in the sphere came to me. One animated shard contained an odd pattern of mine, something that didn't seem to be a memory. The other two shards held memories of my parents. Were those my parents? I peered into the sphere and caught tiny glimpses of my mother on the surface of the shards. The last time I'd seen her, I was five years old, and I'd never seen a picture of her as an adult.

Incredibly, the stone said that these parts had left me long before the ravishing. Someone had taken these parts many years ago, when I was still a little girl. Who would commit such cruelty? Who would break off a child's past? Were these precious memories they were trying to keep from me? Or was it knowledge I was better off without?

I pressed my face against the surface of the sphere and saw a little image of my mother walking up to one of the boulders by the pond. Resting her hand on the rock, she seemed to look directly at me. How did I even know this was my mother? The sphere got all wet and blurry. I pulled away and wiped my eyes. If I got further into these memories, I'd be a blubbering mess, and I feared what I might find.

Someday, I promised myself, I would come back and retrieve these parts. For now, I had to move on.

Wading out of the pond, I let my eyes wander over the Stoneway version of the house for a minute before calling Skylar's name, looking for her parts. I zoomed along a country road with stone walls and woods on one side. Suddenly, a city rose up around me. Stone skyscrapers towered on either side. The street was devoid of cars and the sidewalks were empty. I pulled into an intersection where the traffic lights were glass. They glittered and jangled on their poles. I called Skylar's name again and thought that if only Skylar's parts could be vacuumed up and stored in the stone I was touching back in England, this would be easy. The pieces of glass rattled from their poles and disappeared into my hand.

Most of Skylar's memories were as mundane as mine, but some others, wow — so many girlfriends, so much sex, and me unable to look away. I was pretty sure Skylar would be happier without a couple of the gf memories, but that's not the kind of decision you can make for another person, is it? And anyway, I didn't know how to throw memories out once I'd captured them.

Aside from the embarrassment of getting in another person's intimacies, collecting missing parts was no problem. Bowl was all worked up for nothing.

Calling Jade's name, I soon found myself in a field of glass plants, all rattling as though a thousand cabinets full of plates and glasses were shaking in an earthquake. I thought that if only Jade's parts could be harvested like crops from a field, I could quickly store them in the stone I was touching back in England. I sped through the field like a harvesting combine. Most of the plants whirled into my hand and disappeared.

If Skylar had a lot of girlfriends, that was nothing compared to Jade's boyfriends. What people say about the 1960s is no exaggeration.

When I'd covered the entire field, many glass plants were left standing here and there. I knew who they belonged to. I called Bryce's name and thought of vacuuming his parts into his stone. I zoomed through the field again, collecting these parts that had been intermingled with Jade's parts. This was so easy. I mean, I cringed at some of the "I dare you" challenges from other boys that led to calamities in the man's childhood and wanted to run and hide from several dates he had in high school. Also hard to take was the moment he and I met for the first time, when he tried to imagine me without the T-shirt and shorts I was wearing. Men really do that? Otherwise, I was forced to enjoy a lot of non-vegan Cajun food that he ate in New Orleans, and I got to see Carlsbad Caverns.

I called Jade's name again to see if any of her parts were still missing and moved on. That's when I hit my first chasm. I was rolling along nicely, when the ground disappeared from under me. Plunging into darkness, I dropped for several seconds — enough time to think that if only I could fly like a hummingbird, I'd be okay. My descent slowed, but then I felt squeezed and my clothes were ripped at by a tornado. A kind of reverse bang went off in my face, and I was sitting on sand next to a stone wall. The stone was the same color as the sand, and unlike all the previous strange stuff I'd seen in the past couple of hours, this stone and sand seemed real. I looked at my hands. This all looked and felt physical. It was beastly hot.

A shout to my right made me jump, and I turned to see a man in buff-colored robes with several goats. He was calling to someone. Soon two men in desert camo sprinted around the corner of the stone wall, pointing automatic weapons at me. I held up my hands. They yelled at me in an Arabic-sounding language. I gave them back a puzzled shrug.

They made me walk in the direction from which they'd come, and I found myself in a little military camp. A half dozen tents were set up around a truck. They used zip ties to fasten me to the bumper of the truck and went around to the other side of the camp, where they talked to somebody on a radio. One soldier was left to guard me. He looked to be about 14 years old.

I thought that if only I could fly away like a helicopter, I'd go back to collecting parts. Nothing happened. I didn't seem to be in the Stoneway anymore. I was back in the real world, and it was crazier than being in the rocks. Was my real body still back by the Ullswater gateway? Or was I wearing some kind of loaner body from the Stoneway? If something bad happened to me, something really bad, like getting shot, would I be dead?

A slightly older soldier joined the 14 year old. I didn't like the way this new guy was eying me. He walked over and began asking me questions that I couldn't understand.

"English?" I said.

"You are Inglaterra?" he asked.

"American," I replied and immediately regretted it.

His eyes narrowed. "America spy." He said something to the younger guy and went off toward the man talking on the radio.

I gestured to the kid that I needed to pee. I hoped I was doing it in a way that looked shy, and it did take him a minute to realize what I was trying to get across. I pointed toward the far corner of the stone wall and gave him a pleading look. He called over a man who looked like an officer, who cut the zip tie around my wrists. They indicated I could go over to the wall, and it was clear they were happy to be an audience for whatever I wanted to do there. For my part, I was happy to let them watch me vanish.

With my hand on the wall, I chanted the key to the Stoneway. In a flash I was squeezed and launched away into the stone. The bang of the passage made me worry that one of the soldiers had shot at me. I couldn't find any holes in myself.

To finish collecting Jade's missing parts, I drove through fields and warehouses gyrating with glassy shards. Twice more I fell into chasms but didn't encounter people on the outside, so I was able to get right back into the Stoneway.

The fourth chasm I fell into plopped me somewhere above 21,000 feet on the south flank of Mount Everest. That's the "logic" of the Stoneway: Falling into a chasm can land you 21,000 feet up the side of the world's tallest mountain. I knew where I was because I happened to pop out next to some nice folks who were in a jam, though not nearly as big a jam as I was. After all, they had a tent and warm clothing.

The Stoneway flung me out on the icy mountainside with only my fancy new raincoat for protection against a raging gale that pummeled me with snow and sleet. Safety tip: Do not climb Everest wearing jeans and a raincoat, even if the raincoat is genuine Gore-Tex. Sure, it will keep you dry, but in minutes you'll be a freeze-dried cadaver. The wind-chill factor was awesome.

I survived because a Swiss climbing team was trapped in that spot by the foul weather. When I came shooting out of the rock, one of the climbers instinctively yanked me into their emergency tent. The blizzard outside was so extreme, the guy didn't realize who he'd yanked into the tent until a few minutes later, and by then I was nearly frozen. Four Swiss guys and a Sherpa wasted a good minute staring at me in disbelief.

"That makes no sense," one of them said, pointing at my raincoat. At least, I think that's what *"Mi piace il tuo impermeabile"* means in Italian. The rest nodded, dumbfounded, before noticing that I was about to freeze to death. They sandwiched me in the center of the group to keep me from getting any colder as we lay under the wildly flapping dome of the little tent. When the wind eased up for a few minutes, two of the climbers unzipped their parkas and held me against their bodies on either side. I suspect they weren't acting entirely out of gallantry, but I was not about to complain. Now and then they gave me shots of oxygen and fed me chocolate, a regular orgy of survival activities.

Being Swiss, they spoke something like 20 languages between them. They tried them all on me, and I pretended to understand none of them. Fortunately, the roaring of the wind left little opportunity for chit chat. One of the climbers risked frostbite by removing his mittens long enough to take photographs of me. I contorted my face like a demented person so I couldn't be identified when this was all over.

When would this be all over? I had plenty of time to wonder as I lay there in the Swiss sandwich hour after hour. What was Bowl thinking after all this time? I was pretty sure I hadn't left my body behind when I entered the Stoneway. Was he relieved or alarmed when he saw my body go into the stone? He thought taking my body along would be safer, but without training, was that still true? Lying in that freezing, wind-pummeled tent at the top of the world, I wasn't so sure.

After 14 hours of thrashing wind, the storm let up and the sun broke through. When the climbers unzipped the tent flap, I peeked out. The world outside was dazzling, the most spectacular view I'd ever seen.

Other members of the Swiss team were already on their way from the nearby base camp, which turned out to be only a few hundred yards down slope. When they arrived, I'd be stuck with this bunch. They'd insist on getting me to a doctor and figuring out who I was and how I'd got there. I'd be the mysterious abominable snow-woman. Once again, I was without a passport.

While my new friends were greeting their teammates from base camp, I leaned out of the tent with a sleeping bag around me. An outcropping of rock stuck out of the snow just a few yards away.

The snow was soft and deep, but I leapt into it, flailing forward as best I could.

Most of the snow turned out to be firm. The wind must have scoured away the fluffy stuff. But I was weak as a kitten from lack of sleep and gasping for breath in the thin air. The few yards to the rock felt like a marathon. After a couple of steps, I couldn't feel my feet. With the climbers shouting at me in several languages, I got my hand on the rock and chanted the key to the Stoneway through chattering teeth.

Blammo, I whooshed into the stone and was flying along like a drunk butterfly, up and down and sideways. I thought that if I could fly like an eagle, that would be better. My movement smoothed out. Still, my head was spinning. I had to get out of this stone world and back to someplace safe.

I had no idea where I was in the Stoneway, no idea of the path that might take me back to the overhang of rock from which I'd started. As I soared above a landscape of rolling hills, all covered in patches of flowers whose colors were impossibly intense, I imagined I was hiking up from the Ullswater along the Aira Beck. A peak of broken rock reared above me. Bowl the giant was waiting for me by the overhang. If only I could fly to that outcrop of rock and alight there. "Hayley West," I called into the sky.

Nothing changed. I continued to glide through the air, gradually losing altitude. I landed on a hillside among pink flowers made of dragonfly wings. I knelt on the ground, exhausted, wondering what to do now.

The obvious solution was to do what I'd been doing my whole life: talk to the rocks. I figured everything around me was actually patterns in the rock, so I put my hands on the ground, my fingers twined among the dragonfly flowers, and felt for impressions.

Like waves on a beach, the patterns in the stone swirled and folded back on themselves. Repeating, repeating. Everything happens by habit, the Stoneway told me. The future looks like nothing so much as the past.

If only my present could loop back to become my past. If only I could return to the place from which I began.

The world slowly shifted around me. Somehow, I was standing still, and the Stoneway was rotating past me, as though I were in the center of a clock whose hands were turning back. Future was becoming past, and at some point in my past, I was under an overhang of rock a few miles up a winding path from the Ullswater. The world of the Stoneway flew past in a blur. Then, it slowed and stopped with a slight shudder.

The squeezing began, the ripping wind swirled, the reverse bang sounded in my ears. And there I was, lying on the blanket that Bowl had put down for me — how long ago? How many days? The blanket was soaking wet. The two stones imprinted with Jade and Bryce were lying on the broken rock. Everything was dripping with rain. I struggled up onto one knee. Bowl was nowhere to be seen. He'd given up on me.

Getting laboriously to my feet, I staggered around the shallow pool, trying to remember the path back to the cottage. The way was downhill. That was good. No energy to walk uphill. I placed one foot in front of the other. I could barely feel my feet, which couldn't be right, could it? Everything was quiet except the crunch of my own footsteps on the gravel path, the pattering of rain, the squawking of crows.

There was the cottage. Bowl was standing in the open door. He was looking down the mountain. I crunched through another patch of gravel, one foot in front of the other. Bowl turned my way, and his scary face lit up with joy. He bounded down the two steps from his doorway and caught me up in a bear hug. I was so happy to see him. So happy.

"I knew you'd make it!" he whispered in my ear.

He released me from his enormous grip, and I collapsed on the ground.

Chapter 22

They say that every decision you make brings you to the present moment. Throughout your life, you follow a path that extends beneath your feet with every step taken. The next step might be clear. If you are on a ladder, place your foot on the next rung, up or down.

But say you are walking down a hallway in a building. You may continue down the hallway until it ends. Or along the way, turn left into an empty room. Then carry on into rooms noisy with people. Now stride along until you leave the building, meet a stranger in a café, take refuge from a sudden shower under a bridge, follow a deer trail through a dark wood. Your choices are endless.

Some say these choices are the deceptive public face of chance. They say you fall from the womb and plummet out of control through life until you crash into a final landing place. How far will you fall? Over what mountains will you spin?

What if you're only 31 years old, so you haven't fallen very far through life, and you find yourself side-slipping toward a rocky hillside, high above the ground? You know you're about to crash into the rocks.

No more choices remain, if you ever had real choices. Finally, you know. Your fate is clear.

And then, what if some unexpected grace lifts you up? What if you hover for a moment in awe of the wind, only to discover that your own wings bear you up, wings you never knew you had? Wings made of magic?

# # #

I awoke in near darkness. A quarter moon shone through the wavy glass of a four-pane window. The wooden frame of the window was white. A clear bottle on the windowsill held three tiny white flowers.

The room was barely big enough for the narrow bed in which I lay, along with a small wooden table next to me. The faint outline of a dresser was just visible at the end of the room. A door to my right was closed.

Laying my head back on the pillow, I pulled the heavy covers up over my chin. The room was cold but nothing like as cold as that tent on Everest, which had surely been a dream. So many strange dreams. My breath came and went, my eyes roamed the room, and yet my body felt far away from me. Did I still exist? I closed my eyes.

# # #

When I opened my eyes again, pale sunlight shone through the window. Birds made a racket outside. My gaze slipped across the rough paneled walls to the white window frame, the three tiny flowers. In the sunlight, the flowers were yellow.

The door to my right was open, and I could see into the main room of Bowl's cottage. An old woman was sitting in a wooden chair reading a book. On the table next to her sat a cup with steam rising from it.

Another woman on the far side of the room said something I couldn't understand. The woman with the book nodded and said,

"Soon, I think. What a remarkable young woman. Bowl says he's never seen the like." She looked through the open doorway and closed her book. "She's awake," the woman said as she got up.

A moment later, my little room was crowded with the two women standing next to the bed. Bowl looked over their shoulders from the doorway. They asked how I felt. When I tried to get up, they told me to stay in bed.

"We cast a bit of magic to save your hands and feet from the frostbite, dearie," one of the women told me. "You'll be fine. You'll just be needing to stay off them for another day or so."

"We'll bring you some soup," the other woman said.

Bowl stood aside to let them out of the room. He put a chair at my bedside and sat down, placing his hand on the red and green tartan blanket.

"These are the witches of Keswick," he said. "They've been looking after you. You were a little the worse for wear when you got back."

I licked my lips. They were cracked and painful. "I've gone all over the world, Bowl." My voice broke, and I coughed.

"Easy there."

"The Stoneway is amazing. You were right. What I did was crazy."

"Yet here you are, safe and sound."

My eyes wanted to take everything in, as though they couldn't believe the world was real. How could I possibly be safe and sound? Out the little window above the bed, wisps of cloud drifted past a rocky peak. A fly bumped across the inside of the window and flew off over Bowl's head, leaving my gaze on his face. Wearing an expression of concern and relief, that face no longer seemed scary at all. I looked out the window. "Something saved me, Bowl. I dreamed I was falling out of the sky, and the wind lifted me up." I looked at him, where he sat towering above me, wisps of red hair jutting in all directions. "Did you bring me back from the dead?"

He looked down at his hands and cleared his throat. "You weren't entirely dead, lass. The frilly-gilled newt I was going to use for the reviving spell is back in the Aira Beck as of this morning."

Bowl glanced at the little flowers in the bottle and back at me. With his huge calloused finger, he stroked a strand of my hair that lay across the pillow. "You are more capable by half than I ever imagined any new stonewalker might be. When you disappeared into the stone, I whooped for joy. Of course, I immediately began to worry where you might come out again."

"I came out in several places. The last was way up on Everest. That's where I got the frostbite. And me without my passport again."

"If I'd had the slightest notion you would launch into the stone like that, I'd have filled your pockets with items you might need. That said, I would never have thought it possible to take a garment such as that fancy modern raincoat you were wearing. Stonewalkers are supposed to wear a robe woven of flax that's easy to slip into the gateway."

I tried to raise myself on one elbow and fell back. "I didn't do anything right. I see why you insisted that I get training. There's so much to know about the Stoneway, so much that can go wrong."

As I was telling Bowl about what I did in the Stoneway, one of the Keswick witches brought in a steaming bowl of soup. "Here's some lovely magical soup that Wanda made. And when I say it's magical, I mean it's magical how good it tastes *and* it will help replenish your magic energy. You used so much."

She set the huge bowl of soup on the table by the bed. Bowl lifted me so she could stuff another pillow behind my head. The aroma of the soup was like nothing I'd ever smelled before. I wondered if it was vegan for a fleeting second.

"Before you even ask," the woman said, dipping a spoon into the bowl, "this has nothing from an animal in it. We saw that in your energy field."

She brought the spoon to my lips. The hot liquid warmed me all the way down like a gentle fire.

"Thank you so much," I said. "I didn't know I was using up magical energy. I don't understand that very well."

"Well, bless me, you can't go zooming about the world like that and not throw your account into arrears, now can you, dear? You just rest now. We'll find ways to build you back up, and you can start doing magic again in a few weeks."

"A few weeks? But I have to finish my work in the Stoneway."

"And so you shall, dear, so you shall."

Bowl added from the doorway, "You've taken years off your life, using up energy that way."

"There, there," the old woman said, smoothing a lock of hair off my forehead with her fingertips. "I'm sure she knows that, Bowlie." She patted my arm. "We'll do what we can to make everything right."

She spooned the magical soup from the huge bowl, and I slurped the warmth into me. Who had ever cared for me like this? Like liquid love, the soup infused every inch of my body, thawing me at last. My hands and feet felt part of me again. I flexed my toes, and they ached.

Swallowing another sip of soup, I looked into the brown eyes of the Keswick witch and studied the weathered face, creased with wrinkles. She smiled and nodded.

"Here's the last of it then," she said. She fed me another spoonful, placed the spoon soundlessly into the bowl, and stood. She tucked the covers around my chin. "I'll close the door so you can sleep. We'll be listening if you need anything at all."

The murmur of voices carried faintly from the other room. The birds chattered in the tree outside. My body ached in a way that was entirely new to me, and I struggled fitfully to account for the feeling. My eyes eased shut. This is what safety feels like, I decided. These thoughtful people will take care of me and comfort me. Drifting off, I knew I could lie in this narrow bed and let them take care of everything they thought I needed for however long they thought I should.

No way was I going to do that.

# # #

Over the next several days I progressed from thin soup to big meals of root vegetables and greens. Bowl wanted to feed me bangers and mash. The witches told him to stay away from the stove. He brought a border collie to visit, and the dog lay her black and white head on the covers while I stroked her soft fur.

When my feet had healed enough, I began walking up and down the slope by the cottage. I went to the Stoneway entrance under the overhang of rock and picked up the stone that held Jade's missing parts. The stone for Bryce I left lying there. I needed to finish gathering his parts, and I chafed at my own weakness.

Every time I walked past that spot over the next week, I could hardly bear to keep walking. If only I could plug into a source of power and finish the job I started. Unfortunately, *if only* still wasn't magic in the world outside the Stoneway.

And yet, mostly I needed energy inside the Stoneway. I walked and walked, ate the Keswick witches' cooking, ran with the border collie, and grew increasingly restless. I had to do something. I started thinking that if I didn't get out of there soon, I was going to lose my mind. Then I thought, no problem, if I lose my mind, I can go into the Stoneway and get it back. I laughed out loud at that one. That's how desperate I was getting.

After another week, I tried on the flax robe that stonewalkers were supposed to wear in the Stoneway. I didn't find it flattering. If it reduced the amount of energy I needed to walk the Stoneway, I could live with it. I bundled it under my arm and went for a stroll up the mountain.

The day was partly sunny and dry, so I left my fancy raincoat at the cottage. When I got to the Stoneway entrance, I shucked off my regular clothes and put on the robe. I put my passport and a wad of US dollars in one pocket. After a long hesitation, I put a credit card in another pocket.

When I chanted the key and went into the Stoneway, I was careful to go sideways so the credit card pocket was the last part of the robe to enter the rock. I figured worst case the plastic would refuse to go in and rip my pocket off. As it was, I slipped in effortlessly, and the credit card made an extra pop before the loud entry bang.

Immediately after the bang, I thought if only I had a source of magical energy to draw from. The narrow stone canyon around me jittered for a few seconds. With a grinding jolt, I was drawn sideways through the canyon wall and found myself in a dark space that seemed familiar.

The ceiling was built of interlocking pointed arches. At my feet was an intricate mosaic of small stones. A stream was trickling over rocks nearby and water dripped from the ceiling. This was the chamber where I'd heard my own voice as a little girl.

At the closest end of the chamber, tree roots grew through the vaulting. Huge wooden beams framed a door of heavy planks. I had a feeling the energy source was behind that door. If only it would open.

Slowly, slowly, the massive door swung toward me. Through the opening came a soughing sound, as though an enormous choir was singing "shuhhhhh" far away on a thousand different notes. A violet glow from the chamber beyond came out to envelop me. My skin crackled with energy. The electric pricking of it became more and more intense as the violet glow wrapped around me. This was like sticking my finger in a light socket. I needed to get out of this stuff before I got fried, but I was unable to move.

If only the door would close. Slowly, slowly, the door swung shut, the violet glow flowed away, and the sound of the distant choir subsided. The door thudded into the thick timbers of its frame.

Dizzy now, I squatted on the mosaic floor. With no understanding of how to gauge my personal energy, I couldn't tell whether I had more or less than I started with. Judging from the buzzy feeling in my skin, I had a lot more of something.

Saying Bryce's name, I thought if only I could fly without falling into any chasms. I rose into the air and hung there. While I was wondering what to do next, my head bumped a tree root that jutted down from the ceiling.

If only I could float back down to the floor, I thought, but I merely ran into the root again. I was bobbing up and down a little, otherwise not going anywhere. Had the *if only* magic stopped working? Was I stuck in midair in a world that wasn't quite real?

"Damn it!" I shouted. "Why is everything so hard?" My shout echoed faintly back from the other end of the chamber.

Generally in life, I've found that shouting at my surroundings doesn't do much good, but this was the Stoneway. Apparently, the shouting got me unstuck. I felt as though I was tapping into new energy.

I drifted away from the wooden door, away from the gnarled tree roots that grew out of the ceiling. What was I moving toward? The sound of my voice had echoed, so the chamber must have a wall of some kind at its far end.

It turned out to be a wall of stone with a circular glass pane set in it. A couple of yards wide, the pane was held in place by a thick brass ring like a gigantic port hole, green with corrosion. The hexagonal bolt heads around its circumference were a couple of inches wide. Water dripped from some of these bolts, leaving green trails along the stone.

Once I moved beyond the tree roots from the ceiling I could see through the pane of glass into crystal clear water. Sun rays penetrated the surface 50 feet above, and fish swam here and there. As I got closer, I saw I was almost level with a sandy bottom, where schools of fish hovered around a long-dead tree limb. White stone walls curved away on either side of the glass and met in the distance. This was a large sink hole, and a lovely view, but I was still stuck in my stone chamber with no way out.

Drifting along now at a pretty good clip, I reached the glass and put my palm against the damp surface to slow down. The glass was cool to the touch, and my movement did not slow. I put both hands on the glass. Whatever force was driving me along pressed me against the pane. Did this force have enough strength to smash me into a thin layer of Hayley goo? Or would the glass break before that happened? If only I could simply pass through.

The force pressing me against the glass only increased. "Damn it!" I shouted.

Once again, shouting saved the day. I passed through the glass with a painful surge and a squeak before I could catch a good breath. The water was cool but not frigid. I swam for the surface with my flax robe billowing around me but only went a couple of feet because the robe was stuck to the glass. I turned around and tugged. The pocket holding my emergency credit card was still in the glass. It wouldn't go through. This was turning into an emergency, and the credit card wasn't helping.

As I was unbuttoning the robe to get out of it, a school of fish ran into me hard enough to shove me against the glass. I fumbled at the next button and kicked myself sideways in the water. If only the credit card would fall out of my pocket, damn it!

That worked without the shouting, which I figured might be hard under water. The credit card jiggled out of my pocket on the other side of the glass, and the robe came free. I kicked for the surface, but the fish hit me again, much harder this time.

My heart was pounding, and my lungs were about to burst. I ran through several if-only/damn-it possibilities for getting rid of fish. None worked. The fish swam around me and seemed determined to keep me under water. If only I could breathe underwater!

Whether that worked magically or I could always have breathed underwater, I don't know. In any case, I couldn't hold my breath any longer and gave up. I took a breath and did not drown. I took big panting breaths for a few minutes as I hung there in the water getting battered by the fish.

That's when I noticed they weren't really fish. They were shards of silvery glass shaped like fish. They had to be Bryce's missing parts, and that's why they were coming to me. I thought of the stone with Bryce's imprint back at the entrance to the Stoneway and held out my hand to capture the silvery fish. If only my hand were a net. They swam in circles around me and disappeared into my hand. Scads of fish went through at once, blurring together in overlapping impressions, which was good because many of them felt unpleasant. More fish streamed out of caves in the side of the sink hole and came toward me in swirling schools.

Perhaps I'm an impatient person, I don't know, but after nearly an hour of vacuuming up fish, I felt as though I'd done it just about enough and was thinking that Bryce might have to get along without the rest of them. How could he lose so many parts?

Thinking about my future becoming my past, I felt myself connecting to the point from which I started, several miles up the Aira Beck. The water began to shift past me. The eyes of the little silvery-glass fish went wide. They swam faster. The bigger ones opened their jaws to reveal rows of glassy jagged teeth. If only I went back slowly enough to keep the fish happy! That seemed the prudent option.

The water thrashed for a few more minutes, busy with fish, and then it was still. I was suspended alone in the clear water.

As I turned everything back to my past at the Stoneway entrance, the water flowed smoothly around me. I once again slid through the pane of glass. Gliding across the stone chamber, I reached down and picked up my emergency credit card. I was ready for anything, ready to go home.

Chapter 23

"What sort of a man kills somebody and remembers the murder from the victim's point of view?" I asked Skylar, as I threw my pack in the back seat of her car.

She put my suitcase in the trunk. "I can't even deal with the first half of your question," she said. "What sort of a man kills somebody?" We got in the car.

"Bryce turned out to be the sort of man who's stranger than we ever knew. I checked the memories of the murder in Bryce's stone — the memories I gathered in the Stoneway — and they're all from the point of view of Lucan Gunter, the guy who was murdered. How twisted is that?"

"Those memories were the ones knocked loose when Bryce did all that ravishing, so maybe they got flipped in the process."

"Well, it was all done by magic, so trying to make sense of it is a waste of time, I suppose."

"However strange Bryce might be, he's not magic. We're sure of that?"

"Pretty sure," I said. "But I really didn't fish around in Bryce's memories all that much. You'd think eavesdropping on another person's experiences would be kind of fun, but it's way too intimate for me. You're right in there with a person you don't necessarily want to be in with."

"In this case, Bryce, who happens to be a murderer."

"Exactly."

We inched along in traffic toward the 405 freeway. Every now and then somebody honked at a car cutting them off. A pickup truck two lanes over throbbed with hip hop so loud, it made the window next to me vibrate. Yes, it was good to be home.

"In the memories I collected, Bryce hit Lucan Gunter with the Buddha, and it was Lucan's magic that melted the Buddha. If that's correct, we don't have to worry about Bryce using magic against us."

"Except for the ring," Skylar said.

"Except for that," I agreed. "The blue crystal ring is a problem."

Before we confronted that problem, we wanted to rescue Jade. After my long flight home, I could hardly wait to collapse into bed, but Jade was weighing on my mind.

Before I'd left for England, Skylar and I had gotten Jade admitted to a "memory care" facility in Redondo Beach. My Aunt Melrose was in the same facility, Sunny Bay, so we knew they would take good care of Jade until we could replace her missing parts. In the meantime, Bryce wouldn't be able to find her.

As Skylar parked near the entrance to Sunny Bay, I reached into my pack and fished out the stone containing her missing parts. "Let's put back your parts first," I suggested.

"Will it hurt?"

"For heaven's sake, do you realize what I've been through to get these parts? Without once worrying whether it would hurt? Which it did, by the way. You should try shopping around in the underworld for missing parts."

"Is that the way you think of the Stoneway now, as the underworld? Is it really that bad?"

"Nah. I was trying to sound impressive, although I did get the idea from Bowl the giant. He told me that early perceptions of the Stoneway gave rise to the whole Hades thing among the ancient Greeks."

"Classic," Skylar said. "Okay, hit me with the parts. How do we do it?"

"Beats me. See what happens if you hold the stone."

She held it in her hand. After a minute, she shrugged. "I don't feel anything. What does that mean?"

I took back the stone. Cradling it in my palm, I could feel Skylar's parts circling in there. With my other hand I took Skylar's hand and asked the parts to go. In a second they passed through me.

"Oh," Skylar said. "That didn't hurt a bit. I had no idea I was missing memories until the gaps filled in. How odd. There's the recipe for vegan eggs Benedict."

"Don't want to lose that one," I said, unbuckling my seat belt. "Let's go see Jade."

When I took Jade's hand, she was lying on the floor with her feet in the air singing a mournful, tuneless song about her boots being made for walking. In my other hand, I held the rounded stone that contained her missing parts. I asked the stone to give me her parts and felt the memories and behavior patterns as they passed in a rush, like a deck of cards flipping by. Although trying to "look the other way," I felt as though I was spying, but the memories were quite entertaining. Jade had been a wild one when she was young.

As the memories flowed through me into Jade, she stopped singing and looked into the distance. I worried that she was about to reach up to wipe off an invisible window. Instead, she looked fascinated, then overjoyed, as though she were reuniting with loved ones who had been away for a long time.

When I let go of her hand, she looked at me with tears in her eyes and took back my hand in both of hers. "One evening in Big Sur," she said, "I think I was 16. I was sitting on a rock overlooking the Pacific. I'd come to see the sunset, but the sun fell into the offshore fog. The sunset drowned in the murk, and I thought how typical that was of my life up to that point: so much promise lost in fog. I was ready to throw myself off the cliff, and me only 16!

"Well," she said, sitting up, "a monarch butterfly landed on my toe. What a marvel. Big black and gold wings, thin as paper. I saw it there, like I was seeing a living thing for the first time in my life. It was the most beautiful sight I'd ever seen. And it was the best reason I'd found so far to carry on living in this world."

She let go of my hand and wiped her eyes. "I do rattle on. What I'm trying to say is, thank you. I don't know what you did, but thank you for it."

We explained that she could leave the memory care unit now. Jade knew where she was and hadn't been completely absent from herself. She told us she had felt as though everything around her was playing out in a puppet theater. Now, she would stay put and rest for a day.

She took a deep breath and frowned. "Something is wrong with Bryce."

"We know," Skylar said. "Don't worry. We're going to take care of it."

Skylar sounded a lot more confident than I felt.

# # #

The next morning we found Bryce in the yard where he kept his landscaping supplies. He was asleep in the back of his pickup truck.

"Bryce, wake up," I said.

He opened his eyes but didn't get up. "So glad to have you back," he said. "And I do mean have you." He clenched his right hand. I saw the blue crystal flash in the morning light.

The shimmering green and violet light rose up around me. Black bubbles burst into yellow ooze with a sighing "kah." The ravishing had begun. I could feel the pull of it through my entire body. I felt lighter and knew I was about to rise into the air. What was taking Skylar so long?

Behind me I heard her say the incantation:

> Metal beaten
> Crystal cut
> glyphs etched
> light rut.
> Undone
> glow fold
> spell dark
> power cold.

She tossed a sprinkling of the Tannis Beltane on Bryce and me. I saw her walking backward around the other side of the truck.

The light continued to shimmer and sigh around me. I felt myself rise into the air. What if Skylar's spell didn't work? The ravishing power was growing just as it had before.

I had a fleeting desire to run away that drowned in the shimmering light. Now, every fiber of my being wanted to join with the man wearing the ring. The black bubbles went kah, kah-kah as they burst.

After a faint sound of wind chimes rattling in a drawer and flash of pink light, the bubbles abruptly popped kah-kah-kah-kah-kah-kah in rapid fire, and I once again felt solid ground under me. Bryce was still lying in the bed of his truck with a four-day growth of beard and a dirty shirt. Suddenly, he didn't look so appealing. Skylar's spell had taken long enough.

"Bryce," I said, "we came to tell you that the ring no longer works. Also, we know a few facts."

I reached out and touched his bare foot. With my other hand I reached into the sling in which I carried the paving stone containing his missing parts. I asked the memories of the murder to come across and felt a school of glass fish flit through me.

Bryce convulsed in the truck bed as though a bolt of electricity had shot through him. This was a lot more dramatic than returning the memories to Skylar and Jade. Bryce's eyes went wide as his mouth formed a silent "Oh." He sat up and looked at me with steely eyes.

"I know you killed Lucan Gunter," I said.

"Obviously," he replied.

He admitted it! That was easy. It was about time something turned out to be easier than expected. "Okay then," I said.

"You have something of mine," he said.

"You know that? How do you know that? Wait, what do you think I have?"

"Me. You have the rest of me. Give it to me."

This was *way* easier than I expected.

"If you tell me everything that happened," I said, "I'll restore the rest of you."

"Everything? Where to begin?" Bryce tapped his chin in thought and then reached up to wipe off an invisible window. "I was born in Atlanta, Georgia to parents who managed a string of laundromats. Or were they gas stations? Hard to remember exactly."

"No," I said. "I mean everything about killing Lucan Gunter."

Bryce flashed me a fiendish smile. He'd known exactly what I meant.

"You swear you'll give me back the rest of my self?"

"Yes. I went to a lot of trouble to collect your memories. I want you to have them."

If he was missing too many parts of himself, he'd never be found competent to stand trial, but I didn't point that out. It seemed strange that he understood about his missing parts when other people hadn't been able to tell the difference until the memories returned. What was different about Bryce? In any case, he really wanted the rest of his parts. I could see him weighing whether he could trust me to fulfill my side of the bargain. To my surprise, he launched into the story.

"It all started when Jade began acting strangely," Bryce began.

"Not so fast," I interrupted. Skylar and I had expected him to demand a little of the story for a lot more memories or some sort of bargain. All this cooperation was messing up our plan. We needed time to get Detective Nakamura on hand as a witness. "I'm sure your memories are a little jumbled, so why don't you take a few minutes to organize your thoughts."

He frowned, and I could tell he was impatient to get on with it.

"Besides," I told him, "I need to pee really bad. I'll be back in 15 minutes. How about that?"

He nodded reluctantly. It is difficult to argue with the "I need to pee" stratagem. If a girl is willing to deploy it, a girl can get a lot done that would otherwise be difficult.

That didn't stop him from trying to ravish me again. He swept his hand in front of me, turned his hand palm up, and clenched his fist. Nothing happened.

"As I mentioned, that ring with the blue crystal won't work anymore." I gestured toward the ring on his finger. "As you can see, it no longer has any effect."

He blinked a couple of times and made no comment. Had he bought the story? I wasn't sure how long the anti-ravishing spell would hold, and running it again while Detective Nakamura was watching wasn't my favorite idea.

Skylar was waiting in her car just outside the landscaping yard. She had already called the detective and left a voice message for him.

"I told him we know the identity of the second man who was at Deedee Piper's when she was killed," Skylar said. "That should get him interested. If he doesn't call back in five minutes, I'll call 911 and get a regular cop out here. That will get us a good enough witness. I hope Bryce doesn't change his mind about telling what happened."

"If he keeps on cooperating, this will be a piece of cake."

"I have to say, I thought your plan was a long shot. It turned out to be brilliant. It's working perfectly."

"Too perfectly," I told her. "Makes me nervous."

"Yeah, like you wouldn't be nervous if everything was going sideways."

Five minutes later, Detective Nakamura hadn't called back. Was this where everything would begin to go sideways? I had to give up that thought when he called a minute later. We told him Bryce had agreed to talk to me confidentially. The detective had a lot of questions, but he agreed to sneak into the landscaping yard and listen to what Bryce had to say.

Detective Nakamura was good at sneaking. The first we knew of him was a rapping on the window next to me that just about made me pee for real.

I opened my car door. "Did you bring backup?"

His eyebrows went up a fraction of an inch. "If this guy is dangerous, leave right now and let me deal with him."

"We've already been dealing with him, and he's okay so far. He'll talk to me if he thinks he's alone, but he might not if he knows you're around."

"How do you know this is the guy who was at Deedee Piper's? And how do you even know about a second man at Deedee Piper's?"

"I went to Yorba Linda and talked to people. Got the photo from Gret Niedermeyer's doorbell. Look back there." I pointed at Bryce's pickup in the distance. "Does the shape of that lettering on the side look familiar?"

He studied the truck. "Just about. Hard to be sure. So you know this guy?"

"Bryce Alden. Boyfriend of the woman who sold us the nursery. He's lying in the bed of that pickup truck."

"I see."

Standing up from his crouch, Detective Nakamura looked at the pickup truck in the distance as though he might see into the bed of it. He took out his phone, messed with it for a minute, and leaned back down to my window.

"This is the same Bryce Alden who gave evidence implicating Johnny Walen for the murder?" he asked me.

"That's him. You must have checked him out."

"Yes, almost 20 years ago he assaulted a man who made a move on his girlfriend. Charges later dropped. Otherwise, clean record. You say he's willing to confess to the murder of Lucan Gunter?"

"He told me he would, just a few minutes ago."

The detective's expression didn't change, but I could see from the lack of change exactly what he was thinking: *Yeah, right, the perp is magically going to spill his guts.*

"You have some leverage over Alden that will induce him to talk?"

That was a hard one. Probably, it was best not to tell the detective that I had Bryce's missing memories in a paving stone next to my feet.

Skylar intervened. "Detective, you have to understand that Hayley has a special relationship with Bryce."

"Oh? How special?" He didn't smirk. He didn't need to.

"Not *that* kind of special," I said. Then, remembering that Bryce and I had indeed gotten a lot closer together than I cared to, I blushed. Trying to wave away that idea, I insisted, "Bryce talks to me. He wants to unburden himself. Isn't that good enough?"

Detective Nakamura looked away and tapped the window frame a couple of times. "I need a confession that's admissible in court, and I need to make sure nobody gets hurt. To have both of those needs met, I need to arrest this man and have him confess in an interview room. To do anything else, I need to be convinced that it's absolutely necessary."

Who knew that Detective Nakamura could be so needy? Convincing Bryce to confess was the easy part of this operation.

"Look," I said, getting out of the car, "I'm sure that I can walk over to that pickup truck right now and get Bryce Alden to confess. Would he confess to you in an interview room? I don't know. You can give it a try if you want — if you're willing to live with the possibility that he won't confess to you. And then will you find the evidence to convict him? Who knows? I'm offering you a more or less sure thing. Worst case, he won't confess to me, and you can arrest him."

"Worst case, he takes you hostage and gets away," the detective said. "Or how about this possibility: He simply kills you outright."

"He won't. I'm not afraid."

That last statement was kind of an exaggeration. Okay, more of a lie, really.

Detective Nakamura cleared his throat and patted me on the arm. "If you weren't afraid I'd never go along with this plan of yours. Fear keeps you careful. Stay vigilant. If he makes a move toward you, run."

I agreed to do that.

He walked away from the entrance of the landscaping yard. Then, he circled back to a side of the entrance gate where he couldn't be seen from Bryce's truck and waited for me to go in. He gave me a nod.

Skylar got out of the car. I might need her to cast the anti-ravishing spell, but I hadn't wanted to run that plan past the detective. When he saw that Skylar was going in with me, he raised his hands in bewilderment. We ignored him and walked on toward the pickup truck.

Bryce was lying in the bed of the truck, staring at the sky.

"You swear you'll make me whole?" he said.

"Yes. I'm ready to do it. Just tell me what happened as best you can."

"It would be a lot easier if you fix me up first."

"Give it your best shot. That will be enough."

I knew it would be enough when he got to the actual murder. I had given him back his memories of that. Otherwise, I was hoping he was demented enough to confess his crime and still coherent enough to tell the story.

"Did I tell you it all started with Jade acting oddly?" he asked.

"Yes. Tell me more about that."

He reached up and tried to wipe off an unseen window. Then, he told me the whole story.

Chapter 24

Bryce punctuated his account with odd gestures, many digressions, and several songs that were off key and had nothing to do with anything. Basically, the story went like this:

"It started with little disappointments. I'd tell Jade I was coming over to pick her up, take her to dinner, and she'd make some vague excuse about needing to do something. She's always been a little vague. I didn't think much about it at first, but it made me angry. I've always been attracted to Jade because she does what I want. I mean, she's beautiful, of course. Legs that go on forever. Not as tall as me, but taller than the average girl. Long red hair, but you would never call it flaming red hair. She was too chilled for that.

"After several of her vague excuses, I got suspicious. I went to her condo and banged on the door, wondering if I'd find someone with her. She didn't seem surprised to see me, and she didn't seem defiant. She wasn't resisting me. If anything, she was more yielding than ever, and yet she wasn't reaching to touch my arm. She wasn't leaning in to kiss me. She was just waiting for me, languid, you know, waiting for whatever I'd do without expectations. It was like she'd become a young girl again, but a captive somehow, like a girl who has no more will of her own and no regret for the loss of it. She was enthralling and appalling at the same time. And she had this odd behavior of reaching up into the air to wipe at something."

Looking puzzled, Bryce reached up and wiped at an invisible window.

"I noticed she was wearing a necklace I'd never seen before. Even when she undressed, she left the necklace on. I thought it was a nice touch, so I didn't ask about it at first. Finally I asked her where she got the necklace, and she told me the man gave it to her, the man with no face.

"I began to watch her. She came and went as she always did. She went to the nursery to help you sometimes. She sat in the café and drank green tea. She watched TV in the evening. No one visited her. I stood in the breezeway of the apartments across the street or parked my truck a few doors down and sat there, watching, waiting. I started to wonder if Jade had some strange disease."

Bryce sang a couple of verses of "Dixie," though one of those verses was about King Kong in Hong Kong. What was Detective Nakamura thinking about all this weirdness? After the song, Bryce carried on with his story.

"One evening just before dark, I was sitting in my truck across the street when a man came to her door and opened it without knocking. He turned the knob and walked right in, as if she knew he was coming and left the door unlocked for him. I was furious. I got out of my truck to storm in there and confront them. But then I thought, what if he's the cable guy or something? Maybe it's nothing. Maybe he's her cousin. And whoever he was, he was a big guy, so I held back.

"I walked through the breezeway of the unit next to hers and around the back, where there's a courtyard with a couple of trees and some shrubbery. I knew her bedroom window faced onto that courtyard. I went to her window and tried to peek through the bamboo blinds. I could see light coming through a chink in the bamboo, and I crouched down to look through it into the bedroom.

"What I saw was worse than I'd imagined. He was standing in front of her. Their eyes were locked together. He was wearing the ring — this ring I'm wearing now. It might seem strange that I noticed the ring, but it was large and it had light glinting from it, and I didn't want to notice the rest of him. As I watched, he swept his hand across the space between them and rotated his wrist so his palm was facing up. He clenched his fist, like this."

Bryce showed me the routine for activating the ring's power, forgetting that he'd already demonstrated it to me with evil intent.

"The whole time," he said, "Jade's standing there in this gauzy white dress, lips parted, eyes wide open, looking up into this man's face. It was a look of worship, and I thought, she's deeply in love with this man. She's given herself to him. I'd never seen that devotion in her face. She never looked at *me* that way.

"I was going insane with rage through all this, my cheek crushed against the lower frame of the window. Here was my lover giving her love to another man. I wanted to smash the glass and attack both of them. Why didn't I? Maybe because it was all too strange. The light from the man's ring, the look on Jade's face. What Jade was this? It struck me that this was enchantment. He had drugged her or put her in a trance. This man had taken her will.

"I must have groaned then and given myself away, because a big dog barked on the other side of the bushes behind me. I jerked around to see a little girl standing there with this dog on a leash, a German Shepard. The dog barked and strained at the leash. The girl was shouting at the dog, struggling to hold it back, and I was sure it was going to get away from her and attack me. I'd been in the bushes, peeping in the window, and now I was going to be ripped apart by this dog. The police would come and arrest me. I wouldn't be able to get at the man in Jade's bedroom.

"I ran along the building, away from the girl. The dog was barking furiously. I ran to my truck and stared desperately at the front door of Jade's condo. I wanted to smash through that door and confront the man. I wanted to kill him, but I knew the little girl with the dog had gotten a good look at me. She'd seen me looking in the window. They would arrest me for murder. I couldn't get this man now. I pounded my fists on the steering wheel. I would get him, I promised myself."

Remembering the rage of that episode, Bryce pounded his fists on the bed of his truck. Just as quickly, he stopped and tapped his foot on the tailgate, as though keeping time to a tune only he could hear. He did that for a minute or two.

Finally, I said, "Bryce, the man you saw in Jade's condo — did you know who he was?"

"What man?"

Oh, great. Now he'd lost the thread.

"The man with Jade. In her bedroom?"

Bryce wiped his hand in the air and pounded his fist once on the bed of the truck.

"Waiting for him to leave — I was outside Jade's condo. I stared at her door for almost an hour. It was torture. I couldn't stop picturing him standing in front of her, Jade's adoring look. I tried to focus on a plan for how to get this guy.

"Who was he? I began to worry about what kind of power he had. I don't believe in hocus-pocus, but he clearly had some other-worldly influence.

"When he came out, I followed him less than a mile to a large Spanish-style house that faced the beach. He went around the big circular drive and backed the Maserati into one of the house's garages. He closed the garage door behind him even before he got out of the car. I saw one of those security-firm signs in the flower bed in front of the house. I'd have to ambush him somewhere else.

"Over the next couple of weeks, I followed him. Lucan Gunter. You want to know who he is? That's him. I found out his name and where he worked, a big building in downtown LA. He was some kind of investment banker, and other than going to work, he didn't go out much. He got food delivered from restaurants, even his groceries. I was beginning to think I'd have to break into his house to kill him. I had a gun, an old .38 revolver that belonged to my father."

Bryce pointed two fingers at me, imitating a pistol, and said, "Bang." He blew across his fingers.

"So, I followed this guy, this Lucan Gunter, wondering, why Jade? How had this guy picked her out? Had he targeted her for some reason? Or had he just bumped into her and seduced her? I wanted to confront her about it, but I didn't want her to know that I knew. When I killed the guy, I didn't want anyone to trace it back to me.

"One day he left work early and instead of driving home, he got on the 5 and headed southeast. He ended up in Yorba Linda at a house on a couple of acres that looked like a low-growing jungle. He put on the ring and went in the front door without knocking. I parked down the street and walked around the back of the house, hoping to find a way to see in like I had at Jade's condo. No luck with that. This was a sprawling old ranch house. I didn't even know which window to look in.

"I walked back to the front of the house and tried the front door. It wasn't locked. A man and a woman were speaking in low voices. I crept down the hall. At the doorway to the room they were in, I got down on my hands and knees and looked around the door jamb with my head almost on the floor. It was a replay of the scene with Jade. Lucan was wearing the ring. The woman was in a white dress. She had the same adoring look as she gazed at the man. The light glinted from the ring, the gesture, palm up, the clenched fist."

Bryce ran through the gestures again.

"I noticed the woman was wearing a necklace like the one I'd seen on Jade. I was about to get out of there when the woman made a choking sound. I looked back and saw Lucan's hand shooting out a blue glow into her forehead. I swear I saw this. Her head lit up for a moment, shuddered a couple of times, and then she was still.

"I got out of the house at a dead run, hoping he wouldn't hear me. What if he killed Jade?

"After that, I followed him, looking for my chance. Two weeks later, he didn't go to work. Instead, he drove to the nursery — your nursery.

"I didn't have my gun. What an idiot I was. Have you ever wanted to shoot someone and realized you'd left your gun on the kitchen counter?"

I confessed that I'd never had that experience.

"Well, you're a more thoughtful killer than I am," he said.

What was Detective Nakamura making of all this? Before I could get out a clarification, Bryce continued.

"I'd never followed Lucan on foot. I let him go in and walked into the nursery after him. He was with a guy who seemed to be delivering plants on a hand truck. Lucan was gesturing toward the plants on the flatbed and yelling at the delivery guy, who was red in the face. Lucan was chewing the guy out, and the guy just stood there like a little boy, looking down, clenching his fists. Everything about Lucan made me hate him more. He didn't even seem genuinely angry. He was like a teacher giving a student a tongue lashing. All part of a day's work."

Bryce dusted off his hands and sang "I've Been Working on the Railroad" as part of a mashup of songs, concluding with a chorus that began "Take this job and shove it."

When he ran out of lyrics, he wiped off the invisible window and said, "Lucan walked away. I followed him to the herb section in the far corner of the nursery. He squatted to pluck a leaf and put it in his mouth. He took out his phone and typed something with his thumbs. Then he pulled the little plant out of the ground and put it in a plastic bag he took from his jacket pocket. He did the same routine with another plant. This was my chance. I looked around for something heavy and saw a stone Buddha. I hefted it. Very heavy, almost too heavy. I wouldn't be able to lift this above chest height, so he'd have to be squatting down.

"Wait," Bryce said. "Wait. Something's wrong." He rubbed furiously at the invisible window.

What now? This should be getting to the part of his memory that I returned to him a few minutes before he started this whole story.

"Are you having trouble remembering?" I asked him doubtfully.

"Yes," he said. "Well, no. You see, I have two memories for this."

Two memories? "Just do the best you can," I said.

"Let's see. There I was, feeling it was time to act. Yes, I decided to do it. I looked around. Wait," he said, puzzled again, "I see myself. No, it's Lucan and me. That's right."

Bryce swung himself around and stood up in the bed of the truck. I took a step back, but he looked past me with unfocused eyes, his hands held rigidly in front of him.

"I pick up the Buddha now and walk toward him. He's crouching next to a plant. I lift the Buddha as high as I can. I think I make a little noise from the effort. He turns to look. I bring the Buddha down on the left side of his head.

"This is weird," Bryce said, looking around with his fingers on his temples. His eyes fell on me. "I see myself doing this. Anyway, I don't know what I expected to happen, but I never imagined what I got. It seemed to happen in slow mo, and luckily for me it was mostly quiet.

"Where the Buddha struck the man's head, his hair singed and smoked, and his scalp seemed to warp as if it were a pool of water that I'd dropped a rock into. It *rippled* and didn't quite go back to its original shape. I pretty much dropped the Buddha on him, and it was good I wasn't holding it tight because after it hit him, it hissed and melted into a red blob as it rolled past his head to the ground and flattened into a smoking pool of molten rock."

He gave me a what-the-hell grimace and held his hands palms up as though he didn't expect me to believe him. Already familiar with this part of the story, I nodded encouragingly and said, "Yes." Bryce shrugged and carried on.

"So I'm thinking, who is this man? This is no investment banker. I mean, the guy is still moving, which is impossible. He was on the ground, but somehow alive. Now I had to kill him. I couldn't take a chance that he'd live and identify me. I looked around for some way to finish him off. What could kill a man who survived a blow like that? I saw a pile of wooden plant stakes and grabbed one of them. The man was lying on his back staring at me. He had this faraway look in his eyes. I don't know if I was more angry or terrified. I raised the plant stake like a spear and brought it down hard, with all my strength, wondering if it would catch fire when it touched him. It dawned on me that this was like killing a vampire. He had claimed victims like a vampire, only without the stupid biting, and now I'd impaled him with a stake."

Bryce sat down and muttered something I couldn't understand. No way Detective Nakamura could hear. On the other hand, Bryce had already admitted he killed Lucan.

"I looked around," Bryce whispered. "Surely, someone had heard the noise we made. Still no one came. I reached into Lucan's front pocket and found the ring and his car keys. The ring was hot. I dropped it in my pocket, wondering if it was about to melt. Anything was possible at this point."

Detective Nakamura had been awfully patient. Bryce was about to tell how he got out of the nursery, when I saw the detective come out of hiding and wave in several uniformed officers.

I interrupted Bryce's story to whisper urgently, "Bryce, give me your hand."

I put my other hand on the big stone slung around my waist. I called on the parts in the stone to pass through me and into Bryce.

As soon as the glass fish began to flit past, I knew something was wrong. These parts were bizarre. Bryce couldn't possibly be this strange. I felt a ruthless energy course through me and remembered the teeth on these fish in the Stoneway. I caught glimpses of dark magic — torture, slavery, murder. How could Bryce have committed such acts of evil without us suspecting? How could he have been capable of this cruelty without us seeing it in him?

The last of the fish passed into Bryce. I let go of his hand as Detective Nakamura began reciting, "Bryce Alden, I am arresting you for the murder of Lucan Gunter. You have the right to remain silent…"

I'd positioned myself so that I could grab the ring off Bryce's hand before Detective Nakamura came up. Now it was too late. The blue crystal glinted in the sun as Bryce's wrists went into the handcuffs. I'd have to sneak into the evidence room again so I could get the ring for Bowl the giant.

Bryce stared at me, his steely eyes glittering, like glass fish were schooling in his eyes. His face seemed longer, more angular, his jaw stronger.

Without thinking, I said, "You aren't Bryce."

Detective Nakamura looked from me to Bryce and back at me. "Murder changes people. That's a fact."

Bryce smiled a wicked smile.

Chapter 25

A couple of hours ahead of sunset, the sun was still glowing hot above the offshore fog. Underneath us, three-foot waves from a storm way out in the Pacific were battering the pilings of the Redondo Beach Pier. We couldn't hear the waves in the noisy Sea Star restaurant. The place was crowded on a Saturday evening, but no one had recognized us.

"In the end," I was telling Killin, "the murder wasn't about magic at all, really. It was an old-fashioned crime of passion. Lucan was having it on with Bryce's girlfriend, so Bryce killed him."

"Killed the right guy for the wrong reason," Killin said, stuffing a French fry in his mouth. "Then, he tried on the magic ring and got all messed up. Takes a lot of magical know-how to handle that ring; that's what I've heard."

We watched Skylar feed a fried onion ring to her new girlfriend Emma. Following that example, Killin fed one to me. Then, Emma fed an onion ring to Skylar, and I fed one to Killin.

"Orgy," Killin observed.

"Don't get your hopes up," Skylar said.

Emma pouted.

"Not you; him," Skylar told her. They made googly eyes at each other.

"I know a place in Santa Monica where we can go dancing," Emma said.

"I know that same place," Skylar said.

I looked at Killin. "Wanna go dancing?"

"Ah, well, I also know that place, and it's nothing but girls."

"I'm surprised that put you off," I teased him.

"Not my kind of girls," he said. "No offense intended to present company," he added.

"None taken," Emma assured him.

Skylar did a lightning-fast eye roll. She was sure he was a scoundrel. She found a way to be offended by nearly everything he said.

He didn't seem to care what she thought. I wondered if he knew how much I still distrusted him. Maybe "distrust" was too strong a word. I simply wasn't sure I wanted to be involved with a man who admitted he had looked for a chance to kill someone — even if he intended to do it for the "right" reasons.

Skylar and Emma said good-bye and went off to dance. Watching them skip away, I remembered when Emma came into Origins with her mother, Yoshiko Nakamura. Yoshiko was Detective Nakamura's wife, and she thought her husband was having a fling with Skylar, based partly on his ravings about a vegan scone and a "tight little *Finding Nemo* robe." (The scone was Skylar's, but the robe wearer was tight little me.)

Yoshiko knew what Skylar looked like, thanks to the "so-called vampire murder" news, so she and her daughter sat down in the café, ordered breakfast, and waited for Skylar to appear. Confronted by Yoshiko, Skylar didn't bother to deny the charges. Instead, she went over to a former girlfriend who happened to be in the café (having a vegan scone, as fate would have it) and gave her a kiss. Then, Skylar gave Yoshiko a look that said "Get it?" Emma found this thoroughly amusing and was instantly in love.

Killin, of course, was infatuated with me and thought I should be his girlfriend *obviously*. For my part, I was happy that he was unable to enter my house. The protective spell that Skylar and I had laid across the yard was keeping out all magical people except the two of us.

As I munched on my last couple of onion rings, thinking about Skylar and Emma, Killin was looking over my shoulder at the TV on the wall behind me. A golf match had been on, and he'd been looking at it on and off throughout dinner. He was infatuated with me, sure, but not so much that he couldn't be distracted by golf.

Now he was looking at the TV intently with his lips parted slightly. "There's your vampire killer," he told me. I turned and saw Bryce in handcuffs and an orange jump suit being led down a corridor. An Action News crew had gotten video of "the so-called vampire slayer" as he was brought up for arraignment. The image zoomed in to show a close-up of Bryce's face. He no longer looked quite like the Bryce we used to know.

Suddenly, Killin stood up and shouted, "That's Lucan Gunter. That's who that is." People in the restaurant stopped talking and looked at Killin. They started whispering to each other. He sat back down.

"Somehow," he said to me, "you managed to get Lucan Gunter into Bryce's body."

"You told me there's no such thing as possession!" I protested.

"There wasn't till you came along." He looked at me with a mixture of admiration and exasperation.

"So the parts I got in the Stoneway were Lucan's? How could I make that mistake? Why didn't I notice how strange they were when I was in the Stoneway?"

"From what you've told me, everything is strange in the Stoneway. And beyond that, I suspect you were tricked into it. Someone set you up to bring Lucan back."

"Who would do that?"

"Fel Dinaden. She probably suckered you in with that energy source you found behind the big wooden door. Once you'd drunk her whisky, you were under her influence, so to speak."

"So Lucan Gunter was working for her. What were they — what are they — up to?"

"That's what I've been trying to find out when I'm not busy sitting in jail. I know Fel was using Lucan to collect info about magic herbs. That's why Lucan was ravishing Jade and that other woman. That's why he was at your nursery putting your herbs in little baggies."

"Okay, and that's why he gathered all that herbal knowledge in the stone disk. What did you call it? Etshigal?"

"Right. I'm still unclear why he did that, actually." Killin knocked back the last of his Guinness and stood up again. The place got quiet, all eyes on this man to see what he'd do next.

I stood up too and felt all the eyes in the restaurant switch to me. I picked up my purse, trying to be casual, trying to not look like the woman who had captured the so-called vampire slayer.

Killin walked me out of the restaurant with his hand in the small of my back. When we were outside, he said, "No prison will hold Lucan Gunter. Fel will spring him for sure."

I looked out past the end of the pier, where a few seagulls were still swooping over breakers that rolled in the gathering dark as the sun disappeared behind offshore clouds. "And when Fel frees Lucan, they'll both come straight for me."

Pulling me away from the pier railing, Killin put his arms around me. "I'll protect you," he said looking deep into my eyes.

At least, I think he was looking deeply into me. The light was failing, so I couldn't be sure.

As I looked up into his handsome face, I wondered how he could protect me from the magic of evil witches and sorcerers. And who would protect me from him? Did I need protection from Killin Bardis? I remembered the time he was shouting in my face and pulled away from him.

We walked for a while, not saying much. By the time we reached the Redondo Marina, the moon was peeking over the buildings to the east. Boats rocked in their slips, ropes pinging against tall metal masts like a cheerful chorus of little alarm bells.

The mystery and magic continue

After capturing the "so-called vampire murderer," Hayley West is a hero.

Or is she?

A group of protesters say she's taken out the vampire slayer who was keeping everyone safe. When another vampire murder rocks the little community of Redondo Beach, Hayley needs all her smarts — and an intimate chat with a cemetery headstone — to figure out what on earth is going on.

Newt and Improved
(The Vegan Witches of Redondo Beach #2)

Get a free short story about the vegan witches

Everything is going great for the vegan witches until their happy magical lives are thrown sideways by a hex, a barking dog, and a bad haircut.

How can they stop the hex?

Will that dog ever shut up?

Most importantly, where do they find a magic spell powerful enough to undo a bad haircut?

Get this free short story when you sign up for the latest newts!

Go to: bit.ly/veganwitch